A Year To Exhale

Thank You for being a part of the KH Publishers family of Authors!

Kim Harris

A Year To Exhale

Kia Harris

Library of Congress Control Number: 2018906652
ISBN: Hardcover 978-1-9845-3247-3
Softcover 978-1-9845-3248-0
eBook 978-1-9845-3249-7

This is a work of fiction. Names, characters, places and incidents either are the product of the author's imagination or are used fictitiously, and any resemblance to any actual persons, living or dead, events, or locales is entirely coincidental.

Print information available on the last page.

Book cover design and illustration done by Khadijah Beachum at www.khadijahkreates.com.

Rev. date: 09/10/2018

To order additional copies of this book, contact:
Xlibris
1-888-795-4274
www.Xlibris.com
Orders@Xlibris.com
779498

In loving memory of

SarahLee "Big Mama" Arnold, you instilled a strong love and belief in God in your family, which will continue to pass down through the generations.

Ella Jean "EJan" Foster, thank you for making sure that I understood the importance of being who I am, no matter what "cipher" I am in; for teaching me to always love myself, even when it felt like no one else did; and for always making sure I believed that I am not mediocre nor ordinary, but that I am *EXTRAORDINARY.*

Mommy, Hope Sybella Harris, oh, how I miss you! Thank you for your perfect example of love. You taught me the true meaning of unconditionally loving your children; I am the mother that I am because you were the mother that you were. My soul yearns for just another chance to talk to you, laugh with you, dance with you, and wrap my arms around you. Until we meet again . . .

Monee Rutledge-Gadson, my friend, time nor distance could make a difference in our love for one another. Gone too soon, my friend.

Acknowledgment

First and foremost, I want to give all praise and thanks to God—my refuge and strong tower. When life seems hard and troubles are many, I can always rest in prayer and be reminded of your promises. This book would not be possible if I didn't stop and listen to your chastisement. I had my own plans, but you had a different plan for my life. My proudest moment is the day I laid down my plans and completely, faithfully, and wholeheartedly began to follow yours.

Davon—my first born, my best friend, my twin, my heart. If no one else ever believes in me, you will. My heart overflows with love for you, Son. Thank you for always being willing to follow me to the end of the earth and back. Thank you for sitting up late nights with me while I was writing. Thank you for encouraging me and for your simple, laidback, and patient way of loving me. This is for you.

Ashley—my little pumpkin spice, a miniature version of me in heart and attitude. I smile each time I look at you, and my heart simply melts when you smile back. I promise to be the best example of a woman and mom I can be and to ensure that you continue to grow into the amazing, beautiful, intelligent, confident, no nonsense, tenacious, and God-fearing woman you are destined to be. I love you, my pumpkin spice.

Adrian—it feels like a lifetime that we've been on this journey of love together. Thank you for being such a wonderful father; Davon's first superhero, and Ashley's first love. Thank you for loving me for who I am.

Lisa, Tawana, Siobhan, Lavhonia, Tirisa, and SarahLee "Bookie"—you are my very own personal entourage. Our bond is unbreakable and unshakeable. We are Big Mama's girls!

Asia "Ace"—my BFF, my soror, and my sister from another mother. Girl, we've been there, and we've done that . . . if only they knew. I love you and know that blood couldn't make us any closer. I'm looking forward to the day we are old ladies, sitting on the porch, and telling our tales of woe.

Rhonda "Lynn," Shirley "Shirls," Yulanda "Yogi"—just when we thought we had our friendships solidified and forged, God felt it necessary to bring us together and form our sisterly bond. We often say, "I never thought I'd make a new best friend at my age," but hey, look at us. We did just that! I love my sissies.

Delta Sigma Theta Sorority, Inc. - I LOVE MY DST.
We Ready! We Ready!

Special thanks to

Tara Crayton, Donna Stewart, Alicia Singleton—thank you, ladies, for your inspiration in creating the framework for these beautiful, tenacious, and inspirational four women. Here's to our many more years of friendship, brutal honesty, and goofiness. I never want the laughter to end.

Taryn Jackson

Inside of the fifteen-by-fifteen walk-in closet that Tanya assisted with the custom eggersmann design, Taryn Jackson—five-foot-five, caramel-colored skin, small-waist, thick thighs and great ass—stood pondering over something to wear to work. She was still high off the long weekend she'd spent with Chase.

Chase Durr was a wealthy mixed martial arts and boxing promoter who hailed from the streets of Brooklyn, New York. He relocated to Las Vegas, Nevada, ten years prior, to set up his own business and orchestrated the biggest MMA and boxing matches hosted in the Sin City. He had a taste for the finer things in life, which is why he and Taryn were a perfect combination. He had his eight-bedroom, five-bathroom, and just about every amenity you could imagine, ranch-style home built on a five-acre lot of land. He had everything his heart desired, except a family to call his own.

Taryn picked up her phone and conferenced in all her besties to give them the verbatim rundown of their weekend rendezvous.

"Soooo . . . how was it?" Tanya asked in her "tell me *all* the explicit details" voice.

"Girrllll, it was amazing!" Taryn replied, sounding like she was still floating on cloud nine. "Scottsdale was hot as hell but beautiful. The spa was tranquil, and the room was to die for. The Canyon Suites at the Phoenician was absolutely stunning," she continued to exclaim. She wowed them with her tales of the hot and sweaty sex that took place everywhere—from the back of the limo to the restaurant's restroom, the pool, the shower, and the elevator. Her story was full of erotic sexual moments, which she had enough to daydream about for weeks. She drifted off for a few seconds, reminiscing over the warm evening breeze blowing through her hair as she laid between Chase's legs on the chaise by the pool. Then as she recalled just how expensive their stay was, she complained, "Now y'all know once I found out how much each night cost, I was thinking . . . ummm . . . he could have just given me the money!"

Knowing Taryn and how serious she was about that statement, they all agreed and laugh. Mia chimed in and said, "Girl, you needed that break. Between the kids and work, you have earned some downtime."

Taryn sighed. "I know. He is still trying to persuade me to quit my job and move to Vegas with him and to open my charter school. Meanwhile, all I keep thinking about is rebuilding my credit and financial health after the bullshit Ron put me through."

Winter jumped in the conversation, lightening the mood, and joked, "I'm glad you enjoyed yourself and all. But, chick, I'm still mad that you guys didn't bring your asses out here to Hilton Head! You know I could have used that money, honey!"

They all laughed.

***

Winter had a beautiful and chic bed-and-breakfast about two miles from the center of Hilton Head, South Carolina. She worked on plans for opening a second location and sought opportunities for building up her capital to get the project started. She's a very proud woman and would rather her friends "spend the money" visiting her bed-and-breakfast instead of loaning her the money. And selfishly, she wanted them to visit just because she missed her best friends.

"Tell Mr. Chase, next time he decides to take you away for the weekend, he better bring you here! BUT NO SEX in my pool!" she jokingly commanded and laughed.

"Tanya!" Taryn yelled into the phone as if she'd just had an epiphany.

"Yes!" Tanya yelled back.

"Where the hell are the suits you were supposed to send me?" Taryn asked, still yelling into the phone.

"Wellll . . . " Tanya sang. "I ended up keeping them for myself. I needed them for my meetings this week, and I knew I wouldn't have time to go out and buy anything in the next few days," she apologetically stated.

"Bitch, you da worst stylist I know! You get stuff for your 'clients' and keep it for yaself! And YES, I consider myself your 'client'!" They all burst into laughter.

"I got you, girl. I will send you some stuff this week," Tanya promised.

Taryn got a bit more serious as she changed the subject, knowing that things have been a bit shaky with Mia and her husband Morris and wanted to make sure her girl was OK. "So, Mia, what's up, sis? How are things with you and Morris?"

Mia was never particularly interested in talking about Morris. She hadn't been for a while now. "About the same," Mia answered, in a stoic tone, "I'm really not interested in messing up my good mood talking about Morris's ass." She continued, "As usual, he's never home, always working. Even more distant. Claims he works so much to provide for us . . . blah blah blah. Like I've said, I think we've just grown apart. And of course, I'm not interested in hearing him continue to tell me I need to quit my job and be a stay-at-home mom."

"Why does he act like you don't have a fucking job, bringing in just as much bacon as he is? And raising the kids on top of that!" Taryn spit out in disgust of Morris.

"Right!" Tanya added. "You need to get you a dude on the side. I got a couple of clients that would make a good side piece!"

Taryn quickly jumped in and exclaimed, "Tanya, PLEASE STOP TRYING TO HOOK PEOPLE UP WITH YOUR DAMN CLIENTS. WE ALREADY HAD ONE EPIC FAILURE WITH RON!"

Laughter rang out from them all. They loved and respected one another and they always found peace among their four hearts, no matter the circumstances.

"Oh well, I love you, chicks, but let me get off this phone so that I can drop Ryan and Alana off at school and get to work," Taryn said as a matter of fact. They all said their goodbyes.

Taryn dashed through the house to round the girls up, eased into her gray Tahari pants suit, stepped into her black Jimmy Choo pumps, and ran her fingers through her hair. She glided on some Smashbox lip gloss, grabbed her favorite Louis Vuitton bag, and headed out the door. She sneaked a peek in her floor-to-ceiling length mirror as she walked past and thought, *Damn! My ass looks great in these pants . . . Tanya better send my suits!*

***

Taryn Jackson, thirty-six, a Boston native, is a divorcee and mother of two daughters—Ryan, sixteen, and Alana, seven. She earned her bachelor of arts in education and a master's in teaching, with a focus on urban schools and Chicago public schools from the University of Chicago. She is now the principal of a public school in the inner city of Chicago. Ryan, Taryn's eldest daughter, is Tanya's goddaughter. Taryn and Ryan's father met while she was attending college. He was a native of Chicago and a running back for the university's football team. He was charming, funny, and certainly not ready for fatherhood. He was best friends with Tanya's ex-boyfriend Jackson, which is why it was easy for them to select Tanya and Jackson to be Ryan's godparents.

***

Alana's father, Ron, a.k.a. Ralph Kramden, as the girls jokingly referred to him, was an entrepreneur and a dreamer. He was not afraid to chase his dreams and at any cost necessary, even if it ruined his family. He was three years younger than Taryn and was born and raised in Miami, Florida. His business dealings led him to many places and connected him to many people in the entertainment and sports industries, which was how he and Tanya crossed paths. Ron's good friend and business partner Tony was a music producer and a client of Tanya's. During a trip in Miami, Tanya was styling Tony for a few of his upcoming engagements, and on her last day in town, he invited her to join him and Ron for lunch. Ron was looking for a stylist and had heard great things about Tanya; he hired her as his stylist during that lunch.

On a subsequent trip to Miami, Mia and Taryn went down for the weekend to hang with Tanya. Tony and Ron were hosting a party at a popular local nightclub and invited them as VIP guests. The moment they walked into the VIP section, Taryn and Ron caught and locked eyes. They flirted all night long. They danced together, giggled, and completely enjoyed each other's company. At about 2:00 a.m., Mia and Tanya were ready to head back to the hotel, but Taryn didn't want to leave. She was enjoying herself while being the center of Ron's attention.

So Mia and Tanya perked up, downed another bottle of Veuve Clicquot, and danced in their seats to the old school hip-hop the DJ played in chronological order from the 1980s to the 2000s.

Five months had gone by since they'd met. Taryn and Ron were spending every weekend together. He was either in Chicago for the weekend, or she was in Miami or whatever city he happened to be party promoting in. Their relationship blossomed quickly; that's why it was no surprise to the ladies when Taryn announced that she and Ron were going to get married after only six months of dating.

***

Taryn and Ron desired a small ceremony with just their best friends in attendance. The wedding was held on the beautiful island of Turks and Caicos. Mia, Tanya, and Winter were in attendance, along with Tony and Ron's brother Reggie. Taryn was simply radiant, and the love she and Ron felt for each other was captivating. The group stayed for a long weekend to celebrate the happy couple's nuptials. The weekend was full of exhilarating and relaxing activities. Taryn, such a daredevil and nature lover, ensured the group was signed up for every action-packed excursion available on the island—from parasailing to hiking in the rainforest and zip lining. Mia, the calm spirit of the group and nature lover as well, ensured there was also spa time and private dinners specially prepared for their group by the renowned chef at their five-star resort. Winter teased them both, claiming that Taryn was trying to give everyone a heart attack and Mia's palate went from government cheese to exotic cheese. They hadn't laughed so much in a long time; the time together only made their hearts grow fonder of one another. And most important to Taryn, her besties embraced her new husband.

***

Ron relocated to Chicago to be with his new wife and stepdaughter. He decided that he no longer wanted to be in the party-promoting business because it took him away from his new family too often. Taryn wasn't particularly happy about his decision because she loved the time apart, which Ron's traveling afforded them; she believed that absence made the heart grow fonder. However, she didn't want to hurt his feelings and kept her feelings about this between her and her best friends. After three months of marriage, Taryn announced that she was expecting her second child. She, Ron, and Ryan were extremely excited to have a new addition to the family. This was Ron's first child. The pregnancy was a breeze for Taryn, and she enjoyed every minute of her child growing inside of her. Ron's excitement made the pregnancy even more special as she now understood how it felt to have the father of her child be there, excited and involved throughout her pregnancy.

Alana was born into the world on a cold and snowy winter morning, welcomed by Mom, Dad, and her big sister. Taryn expressed tremendous happiness for her new bundle of joy and each time she observed Ron wooing over his daughter. She knew how proud Ron was to call himself a father and to be there for Taryn, Ryan, and Alana. He was adamant about not being part of the "deadbeat dad" club and devoted himself to his family. Things were great between him and Taryn for the eight weeks she was on maternity leave. She had a steady paycheck coming in, and Ron had a few dollars coming in from small engagements he dabbled in with some club owners he met while in Chicago. Things seemed to be OK. However, money began to get tight with the new addition to the family, and the added expense of diapers and baby formula compounded the challenge. Taryn returned to work and thus was relieved that Ron was home to take care of Alana, eliminating the need to have to find and pay for childcare. However, she was growing increasingly frustrated that she was the only one bringing in a steady paycheck.

***

Ron began sharing some of his ideas of business deals and opportunities with Taryn. Each sounded very promising and lucrative; however, all were costly to engage in, and Ron's dependency on Taryn's financial help increased over time. They began living off her credit cards, and ultimately, all the bills began to suffer. Whenever she tried to express her concerns to Ron, he would become defensive, claiming that she was "not supporting his dreams." She began to realize that they were not on the same page and that Ron's carelessness with money and lack of concern for the impact to her finances and credit was ruining their marriage.

After two years of marriage, Ron and Taryn decided to call it quits, and he moved back to Miami. He vowed to be in Alana's life and not allow their separation to affect his relationship with his only child.

Winter Jones

Winter laid in bed thinking while tears streamed down her face. *The love of my life is gone. I can't believe he's gone . . . He can't be gone. Why is he gone? OUR everything is gone . . .* It's been three years since Winter received the call notifying her that the love of her life and father of her twins, Tiffany and Timothy Jr., had been killed in a Humvee bombing in Afghanistan. *It still feels like yesterday when I received the call.* She found herself feeling anger toward Tim, recalling him saying, "This will be my last tour. I promise, babe," after having made that same promise before his prior tour. *He said it would be his "last tour." I never thought that would be literal.* The alarm clock sounded in the middle of Winter's thoughts. She popped out of bed, ready to get her day started when her cell rang.

"Hey, girl!" Taryn said into the phone.

"Heyyy, WinWin," sang Tanya.

"Good morning, Winter," Mia gently and smoothly chimed in.

"Good morning, ladies," Winter replied in her bubbly morning person voice. Winter loved talking to her besties as they always seemed to make everything bright again. After their morning laughs, Winter headed into the twin's room. "Good morning, good morning, good morning to you . . . good morning, good morning, how do you do?" Winter sang as she entered their room. This was her favorite time of day. She loved warm, sunny mornings and greeting her twins. Tiffany and Timothy Jr., TJ they called him, woke up with the biggest smiles on their faces as they heard their mother bellow their favorite morning tune.

"Good morning, Mommy," they said in unison. Winter walked over to each of their beds and kissed them on the forehead.

"Time to get up and get going. Go wash your face and brush your teeth. Breakfast is on the counter."

While the twins were grooming themselves, Winter made up their beds and tidied up their room a bit. The bright décor of the adjoining bedrooms split in the middle by a bathroom and walk-in closet made her smile each time she walked in. She loved the pale pink, light gray, and violet Hello Kitty decor in Tiffany's room and the sky blue, dark blue, and white solar-system theme that contrasted in TJ's room. She was every bit as anal about keeping her own house clean and organized as she was about her bed-and-breakfast. The twins dressed, ate breakfast, grabbed their stuff, and headed out the door to catch their school bus. Mornings in the Jones's household were filled with warmth and lots of love. Winter wanted to be sure her children never felt short of love in the absence of their father.

***

Winter, thirty-five, lives in Hilton Head, South Carolina, with her twins Tiffany and Timothy Jr. She relocated to Hilton Head ten years earlier when she decided to pursue her dream of opening her own bed-and-breakfast. She and the twin's father, Timothy Sr., secured their business loan through his veteran benefits, packed up their bags, drove down to Hilton Head, moved into a one-bedroom apartment, and went on the search for the perfect plot of land to build her bed-and-breakfast from the ground up. Tim was always very supportive of Winter's dreams, and he wanted to do everything in his power to ensure that she had the opportunity to fulfill them. They shared the kind of love that most fairy tales were made of; he was certainly her prince charming. They met at Mia's graduation from Columbia University, where Tim had completed his master of business administration a year earlier and came back to give a speech during the ceremony, highlighting the opportunity the military provided him to obtain an Ivy League education. Winter was so impressed with his speech and the confidence he exuded while standing at the podium. Perhaps it was his smooth and sexy baritone voice or the way his officer uniform hugged his muscles or how his chest poked through his navy blue army blazer. Whatever it was, she was certainly in awe and crushing on him. After the ceremony, she asked Mia if she could introduce her to Tim. Mia, who is a hopeless romantic, smiled and agreed.

"Of course, Winter. I will introduce you to your future boo!" she teased, and they both laughed. From the moment they were introduced to the day he shipped out for his fourth tour in Afghanistan, which was a short six months after they met, Tim and Winter's romance blossomed.

***

Winter graduated the same year as Mia with a masters in hospitality management and a minor in interior design from Georgia State University. Upon graduating, she decided to stay in Atlanta; she loved the city and the many opportunities it afforded her creative talents. She loved interior design, hospitality, and hosting. She was always a free spirit, and her happiness was contagious to everyone around her. She struck her first interior-design business deal while talking to a woman as they were shopping at a local antique shop. Business opportunities like that came Winter's way very often, either through recommendations from those she's provided services to or by striking up an engaging conversation with some random person. Nonetheless, she was highly respected and loved in Atlanta for her modern rustic interior-design flair. She provided design services to people from all walks of life—entertainers, wealthy businessmen, local politicians, and pastors. She always knew she wanted to open her own bed-and-breakfast and used each design opportunity to test the concepts for her own masterpiece.

Coincidentally, Tim's parents retired to Savannah, Georgia, and he would travel to Georgia to visit them often. Each visit was an opportunity for him to spend time with his "favorite girl" as he used to lovingly refer to Winter. Tim and Winter fell in love during their first weekend together and made plans for having a family together one day. However, despite how much she loved Tim, she was very hesitant about getting married. She watched her own parents struggle through their marriage, and at the age of nine, she vowed that she'd never get married.

Winter was very attentive to Tim's needs and made him feel like her king, and he was equally protective and in tune with her needs and wanted to do everything he could to ensure she felt special. When he shipped out for Afghanistan, his first tour since they'd met, she was very nervous. She couldn't sleep for the first week he was gone and called Mia every day, expressing her concern and associated loneliness. Mia was worried about her, so she packed a bag and flew out to Atlanta for a weekend. That visit had been just what Winter needed; it was a nice distraction, and she got to spend time with one of her besties. Mia was as bad as Tanya and loved to shop; she and Winter spent the entire weekend shopping, drinking wine, and enjoying some of the finest dining Atlanta had to offer. Winter loved Mia's exquisite palate and love for good food and good wine. She knew that when she opened her bed-and-breakfast, she would enlist Mia to help with selecting a chef.

"Mia, I'm not built for this," Winter informed her. "I'm so worried about him all the time. I can't sleep nor eat. I love him so much," she admittedly added.

"Winter, I can only imagine how hard this must be, not being able to speak to Timmy and knowing how dangerous it is over there. It must be hard for you," Mia said in a concerned voice. As comforting as she could, she added, "Winter, you must trust God. He will keep Timmy safe."

Winter smiled at her best friend. Mia always knew when to incorporate God into the conversation, and she knew that by just saying his name, it would make a world of a difference for Winter.

***

"Good morning, Ms. Jones!" each staff member greeted Winter as she walked through her bed-and-breakfast.

"Good morning, James. Good morning, Louisa. Good morning, Shirley . . . " she pleasantly greeted each employee by their first name. Winter believed in treating her staff like humans and making them feel like a valuable part of her establishment. They returned the favor and provided top-notch quality service to all guests; this made her bed-and-breakfast one of the most successful and sought-out in the area. It also resulted in several mentions in local, nationwide, and global magazines as a top Hilton Head bed-and-breakfast with luxury decor, friendly and attentive staff, and some of the best food and wine the area had to offer.

Tanya Mack

I don't know where to begin! Half of these boxes are not labeled. I can't find anything that I need. UGH! I should have had Mia's organized ass here to help me settle in. That girl knows how to get some stuff together quick! Tanya thought as she looked around her new $1.5 million rental home in luxury paradise Cypress, Texas. *Nah, then I would have had to listen to her nag me about leaving New York yet again.*

Tanya knew how much Mia loved her and was just concerned that she didn't want to stay in New York because she didn't want to accept the obvious, looming outcome of her mom's demise from colon cancer.

***

Tanya and her mother Joan were always close growing up. She was an only child, and her father left them when she was only three years old. Her father Trevor Mack was of Jamaican descent; he came to the States when he was eighteen years old to pursue a career in the entertainment industry. He was an avid guitarist and landed a permanent role in a famous Caribbean band, which required him to travel often.

Ms. Joan, they all called her, was a fashionista and stylist. She had a mile-long celebrity client list and had been the stylist to many in the entertainment industry for nearly thirty years. She met Trevor on a trip to London while she was styling for the head singer of his band during their European tour. Both of their free-flowing lifestyles seemed to be a perfect combination, and they enjoyed several years of long distance yet passionate intimacy. Tanya was born in Jamaica, five years after her parents met. Neither of her parents were willing to give up their lifestyles and chose to hire an au pair to help with caring for Tanya. However, their relationship began to fizzle soon after Tanya's third birthday. Trevor admitted to Joan that he was not ready to be a father and that he didn't want to give up anything about his lifestyle for doing so. Joan wasn't bitter about it; she loved her daughter and accepted that she would have to raise her on her own. She decided to take a sabbatical from her clients and sought to secure a more stable life for her and Tanya. They moved into the brownstone she purchased on the mid-westside of New York City, where she enjoyed every minute of raising her daughter. Tanya was a miniature version of her mother. They both boasted silky chocolate-brown skin, long and wavy jet-black hair, and coke-bottle curves.

***

Joan never felt the pressure of being a single mom as she was fortunate to have met one of her best friends, Leslie, who was an integral part in helping Joan with raising Tanya. Leslie, her husband Michael, and their only daughter Mia owned the brownstone next to Joan and Tanya's. She and Leslie forged an immediate bond, and both assisted each other with raising their girls. Michael also played an important male figure in Tanya's life as he was the closest to a father figure she had. When Joan decided to go back to work, reengage her clients, and start styling again, she knew that meant a great deal of travel and would require her to have to be away from Tanya often. However, she knew that she needed to ensure financial stability for her and her daughter, and she also desperately missed her work. Her business trips often meant Tanya would spend a great deal of time with Mia and her parents, which, for Tanya and Mia, was the silver lining in the scenario. Although Tanya missed her mom very much whenever she was away, she enjoyed being with Mia's family. Nonetheless, when Joan was home, she and Tanya spent every waking minute together. She inspired her daughter and introduced her to fashion at an early age. Tanya developed the same intense love and passion for creativity, fashion, and design.

***

Everyone thinks I'm running from something, and no matter how many times I say I'm not, they just don't believe me. But who am I kidding? Mia knows me best, and she knows how hard it is for me to see my mom suffer the way she is. Moving around and traveling keeps my mind off things and helps me process what's happening. Tanya had never been good dealing with emotional things. She loved to see all the beauty in life and enjoy it to the fullest. She's bubbly, charismatic, and super funny. These attributes are what her friends love so much about her. However, both she and Mia knew she did not deal with grief or sadness well.

I still have my loft in Tribeca to reside when I'm in New York for fashion week. Lord knows I can't stay with no damn family! And since Mommy is in hospice, I certainly can't and don't want to stay there. Tanya sighed. As she pranced around her new house, she smiled with pride. *I made a good choice with this baby! Can't wait 'til the girls come visit. They are going to love this place!*

***

Once again, she looked at the boxes scattered all over her house and rolled her eyes. *Damn! I need a suit to wear tonight.* She spotted the box of suits she had packed, ready to ship to Taryn, and was instantly excited. She snapped her fingers, pointed at the box, and sashayed over to open it. She pulled the suits out and started doing a two-step, lusting over the six sleek black suits she exposed. She felt like she found a gold mine.

Well, Taryn. She shrugged and felt apologetic. *I'll have to hold on to these suits for now. I know she'll be upset. I'll have to make it up to her.*

Just then, she was snapped out of her thoughts by the sound of her cell phone ringing; it's the girls. Tanya listened, laughed, and added her silly two cents as she enjoyed hearing all about Taryn's rendezvous with her new boyfriend, Mr. Chase Durr.

Once off the phone, Tanya checked her calendar and noticed that her assistant had her booked for a six-in-the-evening dinner meeting with a new client. She didn't know much about him, except that he was a professional basketball player and played for the Houston Blaze. Tanya would sometimes complain to Mia about how she hated styling some of the professional basketball players she came across. She'd complain that half of them didn't appreciate style and only wanted help maintaining their "bama ass style," while the others were so gaudy and wanted to wear every designer name under the stars all at once. She and Mia would always have a good laugh at some of the shopping trips Tanya took with her clients. But make no mistake, Tanya was an expert at her craft. Despite her complaints and preference on style, her clients were always thoroughly styled and satisfied with her work. Tanya felt at peace spending money and shopping—two of her favorite past times—which made her job even more enjoyable. She was passionate about her work and loved all the opportunities it afforded her for carousing with many across the sports and entertainment industries.

Another six-figure check, so I ain't even mad. If he wants me to style him in pink leotards and leopard print boots, I'll find him the BEST that money can buy! Tanya burst into laughter. *I'm so silly.* She shook her head at herself. *Let me lay myself down and take a quick nap so that I'm refreshed for my meeting tonight.*

Mia Scott-Reed

At five o'clock, Mia was up and ready to start her morning workout. She hopped on her Keiser M3i and pressed down on the pedal to kick-start her spin cycle. She loved the feel of her gluteus maximus tightening with each stroke of the peddle. Mia's workout was intense as she found this approach the most exhilarating to get her pumped up for each work day. It was also one of her several ways to ensure that her body stayed fit and toned, her mind stayed stress free, and she maintained her youthful glow. Sixty minutes later, with sweat pouring down her body like a waterfall, she was done and satisfied with the energy she'd generated to take on her day. As she dismounted her bike, her cell phone rang. Just as she answered, she heard Taryn instructing Tanya to conference in Winter. Mia was comforted from hearing the happiness in all her besties' voices. She strutted into her walk-in closet and gently slid onto the salmon-pink velvet chaise that was perfectly placed in the center of her closet, giving her a 360-degree view of all her garments, handbags, and shoes. Mia loved shopping and fashion just as much as Tanya. Ms. Joan, Tanya's mother, also exposed Mia to fashion and design when they were kids. However, Mia didn't have the patience to shop for other people. She smiled as she looked at her fashion inventory.

My girl Tanya always hooks me up, she thought, loving the collection of suits, shoes, and handbags she and Tanya spent many hours together collaborating on. Snapped back into the conversation, she heard Winter chastising Taryn about making a trip to Hilton Head next time she and Chase decided to have a weekend rendezvous.

***

Mia loved visiting Winter's bed-and-breakfast. The food was decadent, the wine exquisite, the ambiance stunning, and the service phenomenal. She took pride in helping her friend select the master chef. Mia was a risk-taker and enjoyed any opportunity to make groundbreaking discoveries. Persuasively, she convinced Winter to hire a new young African American chef by the name of Damien Joseph, who had, at the time, recently graduated from one of New York City's top culinary institutes. Mia came across this young man's cuisine during a corporate event at her firm where he assisted the host caterer and made a few dishes. Mia had a very fine palate and fell in love with the flavors mixed and balanced in each of the dishes prepared by the young chef. Damien had been the master chef at Winter's bed-and-breakfast since its inception and had earned several accolades for his exquisite cuisine.

***

Once the call was wrapped up with the girls, Mia popped on her favorite motivational speaker, Bishop T. D. Jakes, hopped in the shower, cleansed her body, and washed her long curly hair. Feeling refreshed and energized, Mia sized up her French vanilla body in the floor-to-ceiling mirror and felt pleased at how she'd been able to maintain her sleek and sexy curves after having two children. She slid into her black Donna Karan suit, silk black V-neck, T-strap blouse, and Brian Atwood leopard-print pumps. She took a long overview in the mirror and acknowledged to herself, *Damn! I look good with my sexy bowlegged ass.*

Just then Toby popped into her mind. Mia secretly loved the way he glared at her each time he saw her walking through the corridors, in the hallways, on the elevator, and just about anywhere they encountered each other, *except* in the boardroom and when dealing with clients. In the boardroom and with clients, it was all business as usual. Then she thought about Morris.

I remember when Morris used to look at me that way. She let out a big sigh. *Those were the days. We've grown so far apart. Those days are long gone.* Mia took one last look in the mirror to ensure that her curly locks were pinned up nice and neat, grabbed her favorite Gucci Jackie O handbag, and headed downstairs to the kitchen.

***

Mia and Morris were college sweethearts. They were both finance majors at New York University, and both obtained their MBAs from Columbia University. Mia's parents were never all that fond of Morris, although they respected his intelligence and drive. They believed he genuinely loved how Mia challenged him intellectually and wasn't just another pretty face to him. However, they understood something about him that Mia initially refused to accept; he wanted a "traditional" life—a stay-at-home wife who would raise his children and maintain the household while he supplied the financial means. Leslie and Michael didn't object to Morris's particular outlook on the future he desired; after all, it was the household structure in which Mia was brought up in. However, they knew that their daughter had no desire to be a stay-at-home mom. Mia wanted to be a Wall Street powerhouse. She'd revel the idea of being in a position within a firm that leveraged her intellect and prowess to take risk that resulted in significant returns. Morris knew this about Mia but figured that he'd be able to change her mind once she realized how hard it would be to break into and be successful in the financial sector and to do so while having children. He made this very clear; however, Mia would often laugh it off. She was such a hopeless romantic and mistook the intellectual lust she and Morris shared for something more intimate. She always wanted to have children but felt like she could still raise her children and be a successful businesswoman.

Immediately upon completing graduate school, both Mia and Morris began their careers in the financial sector. Mia secured a position in a top Wall Street financial firm, while Morris and a few of his friends started their own, ultimately very successful, hedge fund. Within the subsequent five years, they tied the knot, and Mia gave birth to their two children. However, contrary to Morris's anticipation, Mia's hard work and persistence paid off, and she continued to thrive and progress rapidly within her firm. Morris made his frustration with Mia's desire to continue working, known. He demanded that she stop working so that she could stay at home and raise the children. He assured her that he would continue to work hard and ensure that their family had a very comfortable lifestyle. However, Mia had no intention of leaving work to stay home, and their differences on this matter became the wedge that grew in between their marriage over time. She didn't understand how Morris couldn't see that she was happily and successfully able to manage both her career and motherhood. It became obvious to anyone paying attention, Mia and Morris were good friends and parent partners, but there wasn't any love or intimacy between the pair.

***

Mia walked into the kitchen at the same time Morris was grabbing his suit jacket to head out the door. *Damn, he didn't even wait to say good morning*, Mia thought to herself.

"Bye, hon!" He managed to rush the words out as he walked out the door.

Mia frowned behind him and uttered "Have a good day" as the door shut behind him. Instantly, her frown turned into a smile when she saw Mylie and Myles sitting at the kitchen island, eating their breakfast. Her children were her pride and joy. At only age seven and nine, they were already exhibiting independence.

"Morning, guys," she greeted them with a big grin on her face.

"Morning, Mom," they each said, returning the same grin. Mia grabbed a yogurt and some granola and joined them at the island.

"Ready for school?" Mia asked her kids.

"I'm so excited about today!" exclaimed Mylie. "Today is wacky Wednesday. Sophia and I are wearing our clothes inside out!" Mylie was so excited at the pending "wackiness" she and Sophia had planned for the day. Mia loved how engaged Mylie was at school. She was the prime example of a student with school spirit.

Myles was more laid back and reserved, although just as engaged in school, but not with the same "spirit" as Mylie. "Yeah, my wacky Wednesday is basic," he said in a mature tone, as if being nine years old was too old to enjoy these types of elementary antics.

"Well, let's get packed up and headed out so that we aren't late," Mia urged her children. While they cleared their plates and checked their backpacks to ensure they had all their paraphernalia for the school day, Mia stood at the floor-to-ceiling windows in her skyscraping condo on Central Park's Westside and affectionately gazed out over the New York City skycap. She took in a deep breath and uttered under her breath the words her dad told her every day of her life. "The world is yours!"

It was the perfect scenery to add to her motivation and charge to take on the day. She loaded the kids in the back of her cranberry Range Rover and pulled out of the garage. *Please don't let traffic be messy this morning,* she thought to herself as she hopped on the West Side Highway.

***

After dropping the kids off to school, Mia headed to her Wall Street office. She pulled up to valet, handed her keys to Raphael, and hurried over to grab her routine Starbucks beverage. The first sip was always the best for Mia. It was warm, creamy, and went down smoothly. The barista knew exactly how to balance the steamed milk, vanilla syrup, and espresso in her vanilla café latte. Mia strutted into her office building. There he was … standing there as always, waiting for the elevator—*or waiting for her,* she flirted with the thought.

"Good morning, Mia," he said in his smooth yet professional voice.

"Good morning, Tobias," Mia replied in a sexy voice but tried to maintain a professional demeanor.

"Mia, you know you can call me Toby. All my friends call me Toby," he replied with a huge smile on his face.

"Well, I didn't know that we were friends. I'll have to remember that for next time," Mia said and smiled as she stepped onto the elevator. She felt him looking at her ass and internally smiled, appreciating her morning spin workouts. Toby stood next to her. She could smell his delicious Burberry cologne.

He smells so good. This is one sexy man. Umm umm umm. She bit her bottom lip and shook her head. The elevator stopped on the thirty-seventh floor, and they both stepped off.

"After you, Mrs. Scott-Reed." He let her pass to walk; she strutted all the way to her office, knowing he was watching every switch of her hips.

Mia walked into her office, took a deep breath, and shook off the thought of Toby lusting over her and her relishing every minute of it. Just then, her office phone rang. Morris was on the line.

"Hon, I'm gonna be at the office late tonight. Just wanted to give you a heads up."

Mia thought to herself, *It's eight o'clock in the morning, and he already knows he's gonna be late?* She rolled her eyes and said, "Yeah, OK. See you when you get in."

Mia sunk into her huge leather chair and wanted to cry at how lonely she was in her marriage.

Frances, Mia's executive administrative assistant, knocked on the door and updated Mia, "Your presentation to the partners is in forty-five minutes. Is there anything I can help you with?" Frances knew Mia was up for partner this year and wanted to do whatever she could to help her get there. After all, she knew that meant a huge salary increase for her, but more importantly, she liked and respected Mia very much and knew she worked extremely hard to earn it. Mia brought in ninety-million dollars in revenue over the last year and a half; more than what any of her counterparts had done in the last two years. Frances also understood the struggle Mia faced being an African American woman competing for partner with her male colleagues. *And the worst of them were the brothers,* Frances often confessed to herself. She despised when they attempted to engage Mia like she was nothing more than one of their wives at home. But Frances took pride in Mia's tenacity. She would often brag to the other executive administrative assistants, "Mia is a tough cookie . . . sharp, intelligent, and most of all, very well respected by the managing partners."

Mia was the perfect combination of beauty, brains, and swag. She attributed her toughness and perseverance to her father and her ability to still conduct herself like a lady to her mother. Plus, her aunts Tracey and Joan often told her that she could "run with the big boys," and if she ever got scared, just think of the "ass whooping they would give her if she backed down." Mia knew all too well, as this message was drilled into her and Tanya's head since they were five years old, that they were SERIOUS!

***

Mia hit her speaker phone and speed-dialed Tanya. "Hey, girlie, how was the move? I didn't get to ask you on the phone earlier."

Tanya sighed and exclaimed, "It was good, but these damn boxes are everywhere, and I can't find anything!"

Mia sarcastically said, "See! You should have let me help you!"

Tanya chuckled and agreed, "But, girl, I did not feel like hearing you getting on my case about leaving New York again."

Mia responded with sincerity, "You know I'm always gonna get on your case about that. But I do understand. You know I'll be looking out after Auntie while you're away. But, Tanya, you never get this time back, so please get up here as often as you can to visit your mom."

Tanya agreed, "OK, and you know I will. Love you, Sis!"

"I love you too and was just calling to check-in. Let me get ready for this presentation. I'll call you later to let you know how it went."

Just then, Tanya's other line rang. It was Taryn on the other end. Mia said, "Tell Taryn I said, 'Hi, love.' I'll talk to you ladies later."

Four Friends

Taryn Jackson, Winter Jones, Tanya Mack, and Mia Scott have been friends for over twenty years. Tanya and Mia have been best friends since they were three years old and grew up in adjoining brownstones on the mid-westside of New York City. Winter lived in a condominium—a few blocks down from the brownstones where Mia and Tanya lived—with her grandmother and aunt Linda, who lived a floor above Mia's aunt Tracey, her mother's sister. Winter attended public school with Tanya, and Mia attended Catholic school in Lower Manhattan. Mia's aunt Tracey, her mother Leslie, Tanya's mother Joan, and Winter's aunt Linda were very close friends and lovingly referred to the girls as their nieces.

When Tracey decided to relocate to Chicago with her husband Bo, she wanted to be sure she maintained a close relationship with her nieces and committed to having them spend each summer break with her and Bo, especially since Mia was the closest thing to her having her own daughter.

Taryn's grandparents retired to Chicago where she and her parents, Joseph and Michelle, would also visit every summer. Her grandparents lived on the same street as Mia's aunt Tracey and uncle Bo. Mia, Tanya, and Winter spent the two months of each summer from middle school through high school with Mia's aunt and uncle, and this is where they first met eleven-year-old Taryn.

***

On the first day of their first summer break visit, Mia, Tanya, and Winter arrived at Chicago O'Hare Airport, greeted by Mia's uncle Bo. Uncle Bo assured the girls that they would have plenty of fun while on their break. Aunt Tracey was home, preparing a welcome BBQ for the girls and had invited a few friends from the neighborhood to join them. Taryn came over with her mom and dad. Everyone ate, laughed, and greeted the girls warmly. Taryn stood off to the side and looked the girls up and down, trying to figure out if she liked them. Her first thought was, *they look like they're from New York, with their Big John jeans and Reebok Classics.* She rolled her eyes, but had to admit to herself, they looked cute. Mia had curly, thick, long hair, French vanilla–colored skin, was slender and bowlegged, and wore the cutest little wired-frame glasses. Tanya was a silky chocolate with wavy, long jet-black hair and was filling out her curves very early on. Winter's smooth brown skin complemented her chinky eyes and short, naturally curly, reddish-brown hair. Taryn smiled to herself and thought, *These girls are just as cute as I am, and we would be a caaauutteee crew!* Taryn boasted creamy caramel skin and, like Tanya, was filling out her curves. At that moment, Taryn knew she'd be friends with the girls.

Mia walked over and introduced herself to Taryn. "Hi, I'm Mia Scott. Tracey is my aunt, and Bo is my uncle. Are you a relative of Uncle Bo?"

Taryn was a bit surprised at how proper Mia sounded. She always thought New York City natives spoke using their own slang. She thought to herself, *This girl doesn't sound ghetto at all!* Taryn replied, "No. My mom and dad are good friends with Mr. Bo and Ms. Tracey."

Mia chuckled and responded, "Oh OK . . . My uncle Bo has such a huge family. I'm always asking if someone is his relative."

Taryn chuckled as well. As the two girls stood there laughing, Mia's aunt Tracey walked over and said, "I knew you girls would like each other. Taryn, come over and meet my other nieces."

Taryn, Mia, and Tracey walked over to Tanya and Winter. Tracey happily introduced Tanya and Winter, "Taryn, meet my nieces Tanya and Winter. Tanya, Winter, say hi to Taryn."

The three girls said hi in unison. Just then, Aunt Tracey remembered that she still had a pan of baked macaroni and cheese in the oven and exclaimed, "Let me get to that oven and get my mac 'n' cheese before it overcooks!" She trotted off, leaving the four girls standing there.

That was the summer the four girls forged a lifelong friendship. Each year, they eagerly looked forward to spending the summer together.

Tanya's New Client

"Damn! I need a tailor quick!" Tanya hurried to her phone, yelling along the way after trying on the suits she reneged on sending to Taryn. "Orrrrrrr I can wear those six-inch black Giuseppe Zanotti pumps my mom got me for my birthday!"

She went back and forth in conversation with herself. Tanya stood five-feet, one-inch tall and often had to have her pants tailored to fit her height. Styling in the mirror around 4:39 p.m., she accepted that fact that it was too late to get to a tailor, and she ultimately decided on wearing her pumps. She wasn't too upset about it; after all, those pumps made her calf muscles pop and her ass twitch more than usual. She embraced all her curves and took every opportunity to put them on tasteful display. She figured out the secret to getting the attention of any man she wanted, very early on. Her sensuality earned her all the attention she wanted from any male she encountered. Although she wasn't insecure, she often secretly wondered whether not having her father around drove her insatiable need for male attention and control over them.

As she got ready to head out of her new house, she quickly put her hair in a "messy" high bun—her go-to hairstyle when meeting new male clients. She had her own rule of thumb—when it's business, the hair goes up; if you wear your hair down . . . then the panties come down. Although her besties would get a good laugh at her rule, they understood that Tanya's field of work landed her in a space where the wealthier clientele often felt like "coochie" came with the wardrobe selection.

Now that I'm thinking about it, I should have kept on my moving clothes! she thought and chuckled to herself. She fished her keys out her favorite black Chanel Caviar Quilted Jumbo bag. *Time to go get this money, BB! And don't be late. Can't never leave money waiting on the table!* she thought to herself. BB, or "black beauty," is the nickname given to her by her first and only ever, at that point, love, Jackson.

***

Jackson was Tanya's first love. They met at a basketball game at Rucker's park in the summer of 1993, one day before she, Mia, and Winter were scheduled to leave for their annual summer visit to Chicago. They exchanged beeper numbers and agreed to keep in touch over the summer. Like clockwork, Tanya paged Jackson every day at 11:00 a.m., 4:00 p.m., and 10:00 p.m. He returned each of her pages promptly. They kept this going for the entire two months that she was in Chicago.

Jackson was a local basketball phenomenon and also a well-known street hustler in Harlem. His talent on the courts could have very well earned him a college scholarship and probably a place in the NBA. However, his patience for having money was short, and he desired to have his money now. Tanya knew what Jackson's lifestyle was and was turned on by the idea of being with a "bad boy." Jackson understood Tanya's background and was a huge supporter of her going to college and pursuing her dreams of being a professional stylist. The benefit of being with Jackson was that Tanya got to put her styling talent to work well before she was academically trained to do so. Using her mother's tips and Jackson's money and popularity, Tanya was not only his lover, but she doubled as his personal stylist. His friends admired his style so much that they sought out her fashion know-how and solicited her to style for them. Jackson and Tanya became inseparable. They were the perfect pair. Neither wanted children or to be tied down to anything except making money, which was ironic since they were so tied down to each other.

Jackson virtually lived in Chicago when Tanya was in college. He secured an apartment for her about one mile from campus, in which he resided as well for most of the year. He was always very supportive and encouraging of Tanya's academic pursuits, although he held no interest in school for himself. She, in turn, opened his eyes to another world, and he enjoyed every moment of being a part of her college community.

Everything seemed perfect between the two until one day, Tanya's English professor showed up at her door, looking for Jackson. She was perplexed and wondered how the two became acquainted. Later she came to find out that Jackson provided a source of recreation for many of the staff and students at her university. This knowledge was the beginning of the end of their love affair.

***

Tanya prided herself on being on time. She hit the garage door switch and walked out to her car. *Note to self, call security company in the morning to get security system installed*, she reminded herself. As she hit the automatic start on her key fob, she immediately heard the rhythmic sounds of Meek Mills booming from her speakers.

Look, I be riding through my old hood
but I'm in my new whip
same old attitude
but I'm on that new shit
they say they gon' rob me
see me never do shit
'cause they know that's the reason they gon' end up on a newsclip

She swayed and bobbed her head as she waltzed to her Onyx BMW I8. She hopped in the car, pulled out the driveway, and headed toward Downtown Houston. *My girl Mia picked a winner with this one!* She rubbed the peanut butter–colored leather seats and lusted over her new car, which she loved as much as she loved her clothes and her money. As soon as she jumped on the highway, her entertainment was broken up by a familiar ringtone,

Now, now that I've found my girl . . . I ain't never ever ever gonna let her go, oh no . . .

JACKSON COURT flashed across her dashboard caller ID. She quickly hit the "send to voice mail" icon. *I can't talk to him right now. I gotta keep my head in the game, and he's only going to be a distraction . . . although I do miss him so much!* She sadly thought to herself.

***

Tanya arrived at B&B Butchers and Restaurant approximately fifteen minutes ahead of schedule. She handed her keys to the valet attendant and headed inside. She checked her e-mail to confirm the full name of her new potential client and alerted the maître d', "I'm here for dinner with Jemarious Russell."

Much to Tanya's surprise, the waitress replied, "Yes, Ms. Mack. Mr. Russell is expecting you."

He's here? Early? Tanya was impressed. She was accustomed to her clients showing up fashionably late, at least to the initial meeting, because once they signed on with her, she made her expectations clear—her time is money, and she did not have any to waste.

The hostess led her to one of the private rooms toward the rear of the restaurant. Jemarious was sitting at the table with a glass of water and lemon, eagerly awaiting her arrival. Just as he eyed her walk in, he immediately stood and pulled out her chair.

A gentleman! Hmmmm. She firmly shook his hand and sat gracefully in the seat he pulled out for her. Dinner was delicious, and they spent an hour and a half discussing his current wardrobe selections, personal style, likes and dislikes in clothing, expectations of a stylist, and her approach to styling her clients. They were both comfortable with what they heard and agreed to proceed with establishing a client relationship.

***

During dinner, Jemarious expressed to Tanya that he'd prefer her to call him JR; he admitted that he didn't like his first name all that much. She acquiesced and sent a quick note to her assistant Rosemary, instructing her to send over a complete contract to JR first thing in the morning.

At the end of dinner, Tanya and JR aligned on having their agreement fully executed before noon the next day. They agreed that she would make a visit to his home so that she'd get a look at the items in his current wardrobe as well as bring over some sample pieces to develop a flavor for his taste. She also had plans to take his measurements so that she'd have them handy when shopping and acquiring custom pieces for him.

***

"Good evening, ma'am. Would you like your car now?" the valet parking attendant greeted Tanya in the front of the restaurant.

"Yes, please. Thank you," she politely responded. A few minutes later, Tanya heard the powerful revving of the engine on her I8. *Damn, why is he revving up my shit like that?* A few minutes later, Tony, the valet attendant, pulled up and handed her the keys. She generously tipped him $20, hopped in, and headed back to her new place. She cruised on the highway, with Rick Ross blasting,

Every day I'm hustling
Every day I'm hustling

Her phone rang again with the familiar ringtone, and the dash read, Jackson Court. This time she picked up.

"Hey, Jackson," she hesitantly answered.

"What's good, BB? How you?" His voice melted her heart.

Winter Stumbles

Winter walked into her office on the second floor of the sister house adjacent to the main house of her bed-and-breakfast. She loved the rustic interior design and decor that she and Mia spent three months mulling over. From the color palette, drapery, and custom-made furniture. Mia had an "eye" for decorating, and they all often wondered why she didn't pursue a career in interior design. She and Winter shared this common factor and always enjoyed spending time together collaborating and executing their muses. Just as Tanya was the go-to for filling up all their closets with the hottest fashion, Taryn was responsible for fulfilling their lives with exhilarating daredevil adventures, Mia influenced the chic and classy, and Winter inspired the Feng Shui. They complemented each other so well.

***

Just as she sat at her desk, Winter was startled by a knock at her door. She pondered for a few seconds over who it could be since she wasn't expecting anyone, and her staff always went directly to Joseph, the hospitality director, with any questions or concerns. She curiously headed to the door, opening it with her normal friendly smile.

"Good morning," she said to the handsome gentleman standing at the door.

"Good morning, Ms. Jones," he greeted in return, exposing a straight line of pearly white teeth. Winter just stood there frozen in time, staring at this beautiful, chocolate, well-built tower of a man standing at her front door with a smile that would captivate an audience of women. His chest pushed through the barricade of his navy-blue uniform shirt and mounted the gold shield like a diamond sitting atop a fine base setting.

"Ms. Jones?" he inquired as if perhaps he had the wrong person. Winter was snapped out of her daze and stuttered, "Y-y-yeeess, I'm Winter—I mean I'm Ms. Jones. How can I help you, Officer?"

"Howard." He stuck out his hand to offer a friendly handshake.

"How can I help you, Officer Howard?" Winter repeated in a sexy yet concerned voice, wondering why there was a police officer at her door; although inwardly, she was happy he was there.

"Are you the owner of the bed-and-breakfast next door?" he inquired.

"Yes, that's my establishment," she responded in confusion. "Is everything OK? Did something happen? Is everyone OK?" She began to worry.

"All is well, Ms. Jones. One of your patrons has lost their dog and called to report it. Proper protocol is for us to notify the owner when law enforcement will be on premise conducting a search and rescue."

Winter felt a rush of relief come over her. She was happy to hear that no one was hurt or anything worse. Then she immediately thought about the missing dog.

"I hope the dog is OK and that you all are able to find it soon. Is there anything I can do to help?" With every passing minute, Winter was sizing up the chocolate wonder and lusting over the solid physique standing in front of her.

"Thank you for the offer. I will keep you posted. I'll let you get back to work now." He turned away and headed back down the stairs. Winter sunk into her chair with visuals of the fine specimen who just left her office. She bit her bottom lip and took in a deep breath.

I am so damn horny! I need to get some soon. These granny panties have got to come off! She giggled at the thought "granny panties." That's Taryn's favorite insult when she felt like her besties needed to have sex.

Two hours had gone by when one of the officers yelled out, "Found him!"

Winter could hear the exclamation through the half-ajar window in her office. She then heard the relieved celebration of the owners.

"Snowball! Oh my gosh . . . Snowball, I'm so happy they found you!"

Winter smiled, feeling happy for the dog owners. She made a mental note to have Joseph send a special package of doggie treats and a complimentary bottle of wine to their room later. She decided to head down to thank the officers in person for their prompt response and service to her guests. Winter was keen on maintaining close community ties, which was one reason she often hired locals. She wanted her economic and environmental footprint to be remembered as positive for all she encountered. Halfway down the steps, she noticed Officer

Howard heading up toward her. She was caught off guard and clumsily tripped over her own foot, tumbling head first down the steps. Officer Howard rushed up toward her, catching her in his arms before she could hit the floor. Winter was flushed with embarrassment as Officer Howard asked her, "Are you OK?"

She gathered herself and quickly responded, "Yes. Thank you! I was heading down to thank you and your colleagues for helping my guests find their dog. When I saw you coming up the steps, I was startled. I'm so sorry, and thanks again." Still cringing from embarrassment, Winter nervously asked, "Are you free for dinner, Officer Howard? I'd like to treat you to a nice meal for saving me from breaking my damn neck!" She chuckled and was secretly shocked at how forward and spontaneous her request was.

"Charles . . . I mean, Charlie. You can call me Charlie. And yes, I'm free for dinner tonight," he accepted with a warm smile.

Tonight? Did I say tonight? OMG I can't believe I asked at all. But yes, TONIGHT . . . TONIGHT . . . TONIGHT! She celebrated the thought.

"Should I pick you up? Here?" Charlie asked.

"Yes, you may pick me up here. Tonight. Seven, if that's good for you."

There was a slight pause and moment of silence as they caught each other's gaze. "Yes, seven is good for me," he replied. Realizing they were still standing embraced on the steps, they both blurted a quick laugh and headed down the stairs.

Tanya Measures

Tanya pulled up to the front gates of Jemarious's mansion on Lazy Lane Boulevard. It was guarded more securely than Fort Knox. She thought to herself, *Why do some men always overcompensate with material things?*

She realized she was being judgmental, especially since she didn't know her new client very well. However, she couldn't help her unconscious biases toward all men, especially black men with money.

I bet he has a tiny penis. I'm going to sneak a peek when I take his measurements. She chuckled and buzzed at the front gate. A Caribbean voice sang through the intercom, "Whooo may ask isss ittt?"

Tanya felt comfortable at the soothing sound of her voice and mimicked her as she responded, "Tanyaaaa Maacckkk. I'm here to see Mr. Jemarious Russell."

Instantly, there was a buzz, and the front gates glided open. Tanya drove up the driveway, admiring the precisely manicured lawn and the unique touch of the weeping willows lining the driveway. She reached the front of the house, and much to her surprise, there were only three cars in the driveway. She expected to find a driveway full of luxury and sports vehicles and was certain the garage would be full as well. Instead, there were a black Infiniti QX80 SUV, a red Audi RS5 Coupe, and a black Nissan Murano Platinum Edition. She parked her car next to the Murano, hopped out, grabbed her bags, and headed to the front door.

The glass doors opened just as she was about to ring the bell. Standing in the doorway was JR with a big, warm, and welcoming smile.

"Hi, Tanya! Nice to see you again!" He reached out his hand to take her bags. She handed them over and eased into the house. Her first impression was how clean and immaculate his house was. *Damn, his housekeeper don't play!*

"I was just about to eat lunch. Are you hungry?" JR offered.

She was startled midthought but quickly replied, "No, thank you. I just had a bran muffin and orange juice."

Tanya followed JR into the kitchen. He sat her bags on the bench that was hugged by the massive mouth of a bay window and pointed to a seat at the kitchen island.

"Have a seat. Get comfortable. Water?" he offered.

"Yes, please. Do you have Perrier? If not, no worries. I'll take whatcha got."

He opened the hidden refrigerator and searched out her specific request. As he reached in to grab the bottle of Perrier, he turned around with a sly grin on his face and atop a slight giggle. "Here you go, Ms. Mack," he said and handed her the bottle of water.

Tanya pondered over what he found funny and asked, "Did I miss something? What's so funny?"

Unable to contain himself any longer, he burst into laughter. His laughter was contagious and jolted Tanya into laughter as well, although she was still confused at why they were laughing. He confessed, "I got something to admit 'cause I'm not good at keeping a poker face. I don't usually just have bottles of Perrier water sitting in my fridge. I've never even drank Perrier water before!" He burst into laughter again. Tanya continued to laugh along with him. "I asked your assistant if I should have anything specific during your visit, and she told me to make sure I had Perrier and sunflower seeds," he admitted. "I was trying to be Mr. Cool and impress my new stylist by acting like this was my norm but couldn't hold back my laughter."

They both burst into laughter again. *He is funny and kinda cute,* Tanya thought to herself. Just then, a young woman strutted into the kitchen.

"What's so funny, Jem?" she asked sarcastically, looking at Tanya while she addressed Jemarious.

"I was confessing to Tanya that I didn't normally keep Perrier water in the fridge . . .," he began to explain but stopped and waved his hand as if to say, "You had to be here, or you won't get it."

The woman didn't crack a smile nor pretend to or even care to understand the joke. She couldn't take her eyes off Tanya. Tanya's intuition picked up on the green-eyed monster, and instead of turning to greet the woman, she nonchalantly opened her water and took a long gulp. *I'm not in the mood for no bitches today . . . sooo not in the mood,* she thought to herself.

JR proceeded to speak without one bit of a care. "Nicole, this is Tanya, my new stylist. We are about to get started. I'll call you later." His tone was polite but certainly implied that he wanted the woman to leave. It was evident that she was embarrassed and simply responded, "OK. Talk to you later." She turned and exited the kitchen.

Oh shit, somebody is madddd! But Tanya understood the code and quickly ascertained that the woman wanted to appear to be more to JR than how he clearly felt she was. *None of my business . . . I'm here for business.*

***

Tanya and JR spent time talking about his upcoming game schedule, parties, dinners, and publicity events. She was made aware that he did not have a personal assistant and was immediately impressed at how organized he was with managing his own schedule. Once he finished his lunch, he asked Tanya, "So what's next?"

She promptly snapped into full-blown stylist mode, "First, let's head to your closet. I need to see what we're starting with."

JR conformed and led the way to his bedroom, straight into the closet. Although his closet was massive, she instantly noticed that he was only using about one-third of it. There was a smaller closet that was extended at the rear of his master closet. That space was stacked, floor to ceiling, with sneaker boxes. *I have my work cut out. But ya know, ya girl is always up for a challenge. The bigger the challenge, the bigger the reward! As my girl Mia would say.*

Tanya whipped out her measuring tape and commanded JR to strip down to his boxers, in the middle of his closet. With a wry smile, he confidently peeled off his T-shirt and track pants. He stood tall and proudly faced Tanya head on. She wasn't moved or disturbed by the chiseled frame towering over her. She was a strict businesswoman when it came to her craft. She began measuring his head, neck, shoulders, back, and arms. Then his waistline and hips. Next were his thighs and legs. As she measured his muscular legs, she looked up with a slight smirk on her face as she realized that he had been beaming with confidence about his body and measurements, then asked, "Do you have any lotion?"

JR looked confused, yet was wildly turned on at the possibility of why she'd asked for lotion. He directed her to the dresser in his bedroom. She switched over and grabbed the large bottle of Cetaphil lotion. As she returned to the closet, she handed him the lotion and said, "Here you go. Your knees are a little ashy."

They both burst into laughter. Simultaneously, they both thought, *She's/He's mad cool!*

Taryn Contemplates

Taryn arrived at work and was instantly annoyed by the thought of the laundry list of tasks she needed to complete for the district meeting she'd been elected to speak at later that evening. She didn't mind presenting; she simply hated the politics that came with interacting with the administrators. Her passion for working with children was what had kept her in the public-school system for so many years. However, she has always desired to open her own charter school.

I can't do this shit much longer. I can't stand dealing with all these bureaucratic antics. I love these children, but I don't know how much longer I'll be able to do this.

"Good morning, Ms. Jackson!" a student yelled out as he ran past her in the hallway.

"Good morning, young man, and stop running!" she yelled behind him.

Taryn loved teaching much more than being an administrator. She enjoyed interacting with the children. Their appreciation for the time invested in them was such a huge reward for her.

I need to check my pension today. Need to know what things look like. Taryn had been seriously contemplating Chase's offer to move to Vegas. She reasoned with herself, *Alana adjusts easily to new settings, and Ryan certainly wouldn't mind spending her senior year in HS in Vegas. She is an adventurer like her mom. I could really focus on opening that charter school I have put on the back burner since Ron fucked my credit up! If things get shaky, I could pull my pension down. And of course, I could always get a job in Vegas! Hell, if I can run a school in Chicago, I can survive anywhere!*

As she began to drift off into her thoughts about what life could be like with Chase and the kids in Vegas, she was interrupted by the sound of her desk phone ringing.

"Yes, Mrs. James," she answered, annoyed at the interruption.

"Ms. Jackson, Michael Anderson's mother is here to see you," she announced.

"OK. Thank you, Mrs. James. Please send her in." Taryn quickly cleared her mind and refocused on the discussion she was about to engage in with Michael's mom. She knew it was going to be a difficult conversation since Michael and his mom had been trying so hard to manage his anger issues. He was only eight years old and had had a very difficult life. When he was only five years old, he and his mom watched his father get gunned down while coming out of the barbershop as they sat in the car, parked out front. Then when he was seven years old, their house burned down after his aunt fell asleep on his bed with a cigarette in her hand. Taryn felt horrible having to suspend Michael. She understood that school was the one place where he came alive and thrived. He was an extremely smart child and thoroughly enjoyed everything about school. However, the impoverished state of his family also brought along some teasing from the older kids at school, which was exactly what brought them to that moment. One of the older students was teasing Michael about being an A student and able to read every book in the library but being too poor to actually buy a book at the bookstore. Michael became so enraged that he picked up a chair and threw it across the library. Although the chair didn't hit anyone, it was still considered a school infraction, and for this reason, he was being put on a ten-day suspension. Taryn explained the situation to Michael's mom and assured her that she'd make sure he would still receive all class notes and homework assignments to ensure that he didn't fall behind.

***

Taryn massaged her forehead after escorting Michael's mom to the door. She sat back at her desk and picked up her cell. There was a text from Chase.

> CHASE: Hey u! Sitting here thinking about u, missing u and needing u by my side. I don't like waking up and you're not here. I love turning over and grabbing your ass and kissing each cheek when I wake up in the morning.

Taryn burst into laughter and was immediately turned on at the thought of Chase grabbing her ass.

> TARYN: Is that all you miss?

CHASE: No. lol. I miss ALL of you. I don't understand, T, what is the problem? When we met you gave me a list of do's and don'ts. I do everything you ask, and I don't do what you don't like, so why won't you come move out here?

Taryn leaned back in her chair and let out a loud huffing sound. She had fallen for this dark brown, amazingly smart, funny, romantic, and more than financially stable man. Yet she was still haunted by the unsuccessful relationships from her past. *Things are always great in the beginning, and then they eventually fall off,* she continued to convince herself.

TARYN: Chase, I'm at work. I don't have the luxury of working from home or for myself. Let me get back to you when I get off.

CHASE: Always avoiding the question. I love u anyway. Gonna go play with Mr. Willie and think about your sexy ass.

TARYN: Ditto, babe. And don't play too much with Mr. Willie. Save some for me.

Taryn knew deep down she wanted to pack up and move to Vegas. She was in love with Chase, and he was damn good to her and her girls. But she was understandably terrified of things going bad, and she allowed her fear to keep her away from her love. *If Mia were here, she would smack me upside my head.*

Making Partner

Mia confidently walked into the boardroom, prepared to give her presentation. She looked around and found that warm smiling face; Tobias was right there and ready to cheer her on. She thought to herself, *I love how supportive and encouraging he is and has been through this process.* Having relocated to the United States from Belgium and made partner just a few years prior. He was always supportive of those he believed in. Also, in the room were four of her other colleagues who were also vying for the position of partner. They'd strategically chosen their seats in a passive-aggressive attempt to intimidate her. She found their gazes, smiled, and nodded.

"Brian. George. Loehmann. Kenneth," she greeted each by their first name.

Tobias sneaked an opportunity to wink at her as if to say, "That's how you do it!" Working with him the last four years had truly been a pleasure. She had learned so much from him and earned his and the partner's respect for being a no-nonsense, high integrity, and extremely dedicated associate.

***

Toby began flirting with her just about a year ago, after she opened up to him at the company Christmas party about not being happy with Morris when he inquired about why she was there alone. He thought to himself, *What kind of foolish man wouldn't love, adore, and spoil a woman as beautiful, intelligent, and kindhearted as this one? On top of that, she is sexy as fuck!*

That night, they danced and laughed like two high school kids and shared a passionate kiss that neither of them had been able to forget. She often thought about it and knew he did as well. He expressed to her that she "deserved to be happy," and he "wanted to be the one to make that her reality."

***

All the managing partners were seated at the round table, ready to assess their verdicts from the five running incumbents. Mia began her presentation, and as the last to present, she had the fortunate opportunity of insight into the other presentations, identifying Kenneth and Brian as her biggest competition. Upon completing her presentation and question and answer, Mia concluded that she was the best "woman" for the job and confirmed that by reiterating the multiyear $200 million dollar deal she solidified, earlier that month, with their new business partners in Singapore. After a brief round of applause, it was over. The subsequent two weeks were anticipated to be nerve-racking for Mia as she awaited the partner's final decision. She also knew that she and Toby wouldn't be able to interact much in order to avoid any perceptions of a conflict of interest.

That evening, Mia went home, cooked dinner, helped the kids with homework, and put them to bed early. She needed some "me" time. She grabbed a bottle of Riesling and headed up to her favorite place—her walk-in closet—stripped down to her panties and bra, slid onto her chaise, poured her first glass of wine, picked up her phone, and texted her girls. She needed a good laugh in order to get her mind off things. She sent the "G-CODE," which was their way of saying, "Let's all talk." They all conferenced in.

"Hey, mamas," Taryn greeted.

"Hey, loves," Mia affirmed.

"Hey, y'all," Winter said with her new southern twang.

"Hey, chicks!" Tanya added.

They all instantly chuckled. They knew whenever they were all together, whether in person or on the phone, some funny shit was about to be said.

"So how did the presentation go, Mia?" Winter asked, knowing her girl rocked it.

"It went well. I just have to wait two weeks for final decision. This shit is going to be nerve-wrecking. My main competition is Kenneth's big head ass!" Mia said and laughed. "What happened with the showing today?" she, in turn, asked Winter. "Did you like the place?" she continued.

Winter was currently searching for a location to open her second bed-and-breakfast. "I can't say I was blown away by any particular place

I saw today. Some were OK, but I'm not going to rush it. Taking your advice; I will know it when I see it."

Tanya jumped in, "Winter, I'll be in South Carolina next weekend. Just found out today that one of my clients is performing out there and need me on call. Planning to stay at the bed-and-breakfast. Do you have a room for me?"

Winter replied, "Let me send a note to Joseph to make sure he holds you a room."

Tanya changed the subject. "Don't y'all know JR's little chick be tryna act like she's that bitch, and I better keep it professional with her man! I just side-eye her. Chick, relax! I'm a professional and don't have any interest in him. Meanwhile, he's always flirting with me and has made it clear they're cool, but she seems to be in it for the celebrity. She needs to take that shit up with him! 'Cause y'all know if I unleash TANYA MACK on him, that chick won't stand a chance!" Laughter rang out. She continued, "She better ask somebody. If she keeps her shit up, it's gonna be black hoodie and masks time! Me and my chicks are gonna set shit on fire!"

A thunder of laughter rang out. Taryn added, "YES! And I'm gonna beat her mama ass for not teaching her how to recognize when a dude ain't interested." They all cracked up. Those who know them best knew the four of them, while educated and professional, could also be some ruthless chicks.

***

Mia sat in her chaise and finished the bottle of wine. She felt amazing and extraordinarily happy that she was close to achieving her goal of becoming a partner. Myles and Mylie were very supportive and happy for their mom. They made her heart melt when they handed her their handmade gifts of congratulations on getting to this point. She loved how thoughtful and supportive her children were throughout this entire process, unlike their father.

Myles crafted a picture frame with a poem entitled "My Mom Is My Hero." Mylie designed her a bracelet with gold and black beads. She said she'd chosen the colors because "they were like an award." She was extremely grateful and touched by her children's gesture and planned to hang Myles's poem in her office and wear Mylie's bracelet to work the next day.

If only Morris would be as happy for me. I don't understand how he can be so stubborn. Is it so bad for me to want a career and a family? I mean, shit, I'm smart as hell, a damn good cook, hell of a mother, a hell of a wife, and I fucked the shit out of him each and EVERY time he wanted some. How long has it been since we last . . . damn! Nearly two years . . . what a shame! As Mia lay deep in thought, she didn't realize that her cell phone had rung. She was snapped out of her haze at the buzzing sound, notifying her that she had a voice message. The caller ID read "Unknown," so she was unable to identify the caller. She checked her voice mail and immediately recognized the voice of her Aunt Joan.

∞

> "Hey, my love. It's me, Auntie Joan. Just calling to see how everything went with the presentation today. I am so proud of you and always knew you would achieve whatever you set out to do. Now you go and rock that shit out, just like your auntie taught you. I also can't wait to see you and the kids at the end of the month. I miss you and them babies. And please do me a favor and leave Morris's miserable ass home! No need to call me back. I'm about to lie down and rest. Just wanted to say congratulations and not to worry. Partner is YOURS! Love you, babe!"

∞

Mia smiled at hearing her Aunt Joan sound in such high spirits. She could only imagine how tough it was for her to remain positive in light of having terminal cancer. But if anyone could make the most out of any situation, that would be Aunt Joan.

***

Mia contemplated calling Toby. She wanted to hear his voice. The next two weeks were going to be hard without being able to exchange glances, flirts, laughs, and genuine conversation with her "friend." Although she understood why, she didn't like it very much. *Oh well. Guess I'm left with my fantasies.* She smiled to herself, sat back, and allowed herself to indulge in her favorite fantasy about Tobias.

Open to Love

Winter wrapped up for the day and looked over at the clock. It read 6:15 p.m. *Forty-five minutes and Mr. Chocolate Wonder will be here. I need to get refreshed and changed.*

She strutted over to the room next door to her office and opened the sliding glass-door closet. *I am so happy that Tanya convinced me to factor in this space for my personal use and store some extra clothing in here.* Tanya believed in always being prepared for the unknown. She would say, "You never know when some new 'D' is going to walk through that door and you'd have to swap out of those granny panties!"

Winter chuckled, recalling her bestie's self-acclaimed words of wisdom. As odd as it may sound to some, she believed Tanya certainly had a point. This was one of the reasons Winter didn't resist the recommendation and had the contractors build in a master "personal" space, inclusive of a powder room with a full shower and a wall-to-wall closet with glass doors. This part of the second floor was off limits to her staff.

What should I wear? she contemplated. She decided on her black Altuzarra ruffle-hem knit dress and her metallic lizard-effect leather Christian Louboutin sandals. She loved the feel of the soft knit fabric lying against her skin, which made her feel sexy and sensual. The dress also clung to her body for dear life and accentuated her breast, hips, and ass. Her intent was to show off her curves and sensuality to *Officer Charles Howard,* especially since she was still feeling a little embarrassed at her clumsiness earlier.

***

At precisely seven in the evening, Charlie pulled up to the front of Winter's office site, just as she was locking the front door. Winter smiled, and he warmly smiled back, hopped out of his shadow-black F-250 XLT, ran around to the passenger side and opened the door for her. He held her by the arm and hoisted her up into the truck. He could smell the soft scent of her Nicole Miller perfume and inhaled as hard as he could, as if to take a piece of her into himself.

Winter pretended she didn't feel Charlie inhaling a dose of her perfume. She was instantly turned on.

Dinner was very romantic. Charlie was a gentleman the entire time. She couldn't help but think about how special he made her feel; just like Timmy used to.

On the drive to her house, Charlie was a little quiet. Winter inquired if he was OK. He assured her that he was, and that he was just taking in the moment of being with such a beautiful, confident, and kind woman.

Winter was surprised that Charlie was still single and didn't have any children. *Is he on the down low? Is he a woman beater? Mama's boy?* Her mind wandered while he was talking. Then she blurted out, "So what's your deal? Why are you still single? No kids?" She was shocked at herself for blurting out the questions as she had. Without hesitation, Charlie calmly responded, "I understand your questions and concerns. This is not the first time a woman has asked me these questions. Hell, even my own mother has asked me!" He chuckled and then looked over to assure her that he took her questions seriously.

"I have been in love once before in my life. I met her during my first year as a police officer. She was an amazing woman . . . at least initially. She had drive, passion, and treated me like a king. I was certain she was the one and that we'd end up married with a bunch of kids." He stopped and sighed deeply, then continued, "We were together for nearly four years, and I was ready to propose. She'd just graduated veterinary medical school, and I thought it was the perfect timing."

Charlie stared into space for a second, as Winter remained fully attentive to what he was saying. She noticed his eyes began to gloss with tears, and he was doing all he could to hold them back.

"We were on our way home from having dinner one evening when Angela's cell phone rang. I noticed how surprised she looked when she glanced at the caller ID. She picked up the phone and said something like 'I'll have to call you back. Now is not a good time,' and then looked over at me."

"When we arrived at my place, she said, 'Charlie, we need to talk.' I could tell by the tone of her voice that it was not going to be a good conversation. We got inside, and she immediately began crying and apologizing. I was so confused and had no clue why she was carrying on, so I just stood there and listened. She went on to confess that she was three months pregnant and the baby wasn't mine. And as if that wasn't enough, she also confessed that she was engaged to marry the baby's father."

"All I could do was stand there, shocked and fucking pissed. I wanted to knock HIS fucking head off, but I knew it wasn't anyone's responsibility but Angela's. I started to ask all the questions that were going through my head but instantly acknowledged that none of the answers would help or make a difference. She was lucky that my mama raised me right because I wanted to call her all types of you-know-whats. When I finally opened my mouth, the only words that came out were "Get the hell out!" She apologized again and left.

"I haven't seen her since, but have heard that she lives in Virginia with her two children, doing well as a Vet, and is divorced. This is why I'm still single. I just don't have time for no bullshit. Yeah, I can probably have just about any woman I want, but that's not what I'm looking for. I did my share of dirt in college and am not interested in playing any more games. I want someone to come home to every night after dealing with crime all day; someone who brings peace to my life."

Winter was saddened by Charlie's story and felt an overwhelming sense of wanting to mend his heart. She leaned over toward him, put her hand on his cheek, and turned him to face her. Before moving in to kiss him, she whispered, "I'll never hurt you like that."

Should I Go?

"Tanya, why does he keep calling? What does he want?" Mia asked about Jackson's recent calling barrage. "Doesn't he understand that things are complicated, and you need time to figure things out? I'm telling you, sometimes Jackson is so oblivious. I know he loves you, and you love him, but it's just not a good time for either of you right now!" Mia exclaimed.

Tanya sighed and simply said, "Yeah."

Mia could tell that Tanya had a lot on her mind and talking about Jackson wasn't what she needed at the moment, so she changed the subject to a topic that she knew Tanya would be intrigued in discussing.

"Girl! Tobias, I mean Toby, asked me if I wanted to get a drink after work tomorrow to celebrate my making partner. What should I do?" Mia asked as if she were searching the universe for an answer.

Tanya was instantly revitalized. She loved a good "hookup" situation. "Girllll, I think you should go . . . What's the harm? And let me know if he needs a stylist."

Mia cracked up laughing. Tanya was always getting her hustle on. "I bet if you go, Morris won't even notice! He probably won't even be home," Tanya said sarcastically. Mia knew this was certainly true and yet no longer cared.

"But, girl, what will we talk about?" Mia nervously asked as if this were her first date.

Tanya sucked her teeth and said, "Girl, stop acting like you forgot that freak in you. Say what you need to say to get that 'D' hard!"

Mia screamed out in laughter. "You are a fool, Tanya!"

They both laughed hard. Tanya knew Mia had done her best to be a doting and faithful wife. But Morris had been so unreasonable and stubborn about her career that he all—but physically—abandoned their marriage. She also felt that Mia's deprived freak needed to be released.

"Let's call Taryn and Winter and see what they have to say about this!" Tanya teased and sent out the G-CODE.

"Hey, girls," Mia greeted in her naturally soft and soothing voice.

"Hey, mamas!" Taryn greeted.

"Hey, chicks!" Tanya said while stuffing a few grapes into her mouth.

"Hey, y'all!" Winter sang in her southern drawl.

Tanya jumped right into it. "Sooooo, Tobias. I mean, Tobyyyyy"—she stretched out his name, and everyone laughed—"wants to take Mia out for drinks tomorrow night to celebrate her making partner, and SHE wants to know what SHE should do." She made this statement as if the answer were obvious to anyone asked. "Now y'all know I'm all for the get down! So what do you think?" she continued.

Winter chimed in and said, "Hon, I say go, have a drink, a few laughs, and nothing more . . . you deserve to celebrate."

Taryn exclaimed, "Chick! GO! Go get you some good white boy dick!" They all burst into hysterical laughter. Taryn continued, "Morris ain't laid the pipe in over a year! Y'all practically sister and brother!" They all laughed again. Amid the jokes, they were all sincerely upset with Morris for treating their girl this way, simply because he's mad that she was a "boss bitch," as Tanya would often put it, and he wanted her home, barefoot and pregnant.

"You need some! I can't wait until we get there so we can meet Mr. Tobias Smith. I'm gon' tell him to grab your ass!" Taryn joked, and they all laughed.

Her besties always made her feel happy. They were all honest with each another and have always stuck by one another through all circumstances. Their relationship was a no-judgment zone, which was why they were comfortable being vulnerable with one another.

"Speaking of when y'all get here, what time are your flights arriving on Friday?" Mia inquired.

Tanya excitedly replied, "I'm flying in early. I have to meet up with Lance, my other NBA client from the NY Spikes. He needs me to style him for his birthday party next weekend. From there, I'll stop by my condo to change and get ready to meet up with y'all at Mia's."

Winter added, "The twins and I will arrive by 4:00 p.m. You don't have to pick us up. I've made arrangements with a car service. We'll head straight to your place from the airport. I'll change at your house. They are so excited to see all the kids. Tiffany complained to me that "Ryan never wants to come anywhere because she thinks she's an adult now that she's almost in college."

They all laughed at Tiffany's accusation. Taryn responded, "Tell Tiffy, don't worry. Her big cousin still loves her. Alana and I will be getting in about 4:00 p.m. also. I'm going to stop at the hotel and get us checked in. I'll shower and change there, and then Alana and I will head to your place. What time will the sitter get to your place? I want to make sure I know what time to have the car service pick us up for dinner."

"She'll be here by four thirty. The kids are going to have a ball this weekend, and so are we! I can't wait! Morris was annoyed and had the nerve to say to me, 'So I guess I won't be seeing you this weekend.' I had to laugh," Mia revealed as if she could care less about what Morris said.

Tanya rolled her eyes on the other end and said, "Morris, please! Get yo' life!"

They all laughed. "OK, girls, I gotta figure out what I'm going to wear tomorrow and get some sleep. Will let y'all know how it goes with Toby."

"Oh, so you're gonna go?" Winter asked in a high-pitched and pleasantly surprised voice.

"Yeah, I'm gonna go," Mia answered as if she'd just told the biggest secret of her life.

"Yeah, bihhhhhhh!" Tanya excitedly exclaimed. "Go get that 'D'!" They all laughed again.

"Love y'all. Good night with y'all crazy butts." Mia chuckled. They all say their good nights and hung up.

***

Mia stood in the middle of her closet, mulling over what to wear to work the next day. She wanted something easy to transition from the office to drinks with Toby. She suffered no shortage of clothing but found herself wanting something new to wear.

Ugh, it's too late to go buy something. She knew she wanted something slightly revealing to tease his senses but not completely scream "I WANT YOU." She snapped her fingers as if she had an epiphany.

"I know what I'll wear." She pulled out a black-and-red pin-striped Tahari skirt suit. *A skirt. Yes. Easy access.* She shook the thought from her head, although she preferred to allow her mind to wander about Toby. She then grabbed a red silk blouse that had an ultradeep plunge neck, her red studded leather Saint Laurent ERA 110 cage sandals, and her black Saint Laurent Jamie bag. Mia was pleased with her outfit selection. *I'm going to wash and blow my hair out. I'm in the mood for a straight-hair look.*

Love Is In The Air

Winter tossed and turned all night. She couldn't stop thinking about Charlie. She hated Angela for hurting him the way she did, but was also thankful that she did.

Am I a horrible person for being thankful of someone getting hurt? She knew she didn't like the idea of Charlie being hurt. She was simply thankful that he was still out there, and love hadn't snatched him from her grasp. She was decisive with her heart, and knew she found love when she first saw Timmy standing on the podium, just like she knew she'd found love the moment she fell into Charlie's arms on that fateful day.

I hope it's not too late or too hopeless. I hope he wants to give love another try. I pray he doesn't mind that I have children. Winter found herself anxiously replaying these thoughts over and over in her head until she dozed off to sleep.

***

Winter jumped up at the sound of her phone buzzing. She glanced over at her alarm clock and the time read 4:43 a.m.

Who's texting me this time of morning? She picked up the phone, and the message read—

> CHARLIE: Just thinking of you. Hope I didn't disturb your beauty rest. Have a good day, pretty lady. Always, Charlie

Winter smiled, and her heart fluttered.

> WINTER: Hey, you! Yes, you did disturb my beauty rest. LOL. But thank you, nonetheless, for thinking of me. Miss you!

She hit send without thinking and immediately regretted it. *Miss you? OMG. Why would I type that? He's going to think I'm freaking crazy. I just met him, and already, I'm saying, "Miss you."*

She wanted to smack herself. Although deep down, she truly felt that way. He responded immediately.

CHARLIE: Really?? Well, I miss you too. Hope to see you again soon. Will call you later.

Winter smiled and sighed. All she wanted to do was cuddle in his arms at that moment. *He certainly will see me real soon. ALL of me.* She couldn't fall back asleep, so she got up, showered, and dressed.

***

Winter heard the twins laughing from their bedrooms and was glad to hear they were awake. As she walked in Tiffany's room, she was jumped from both sides. They were on her, hugging her and laughing.

"Good morning, Mommy!" they sang out.

"Good morning, my loves," she sang back. "What are you guys so excited about this morning?" she asked.

"We are going to see Aunty Mia and Uncle Morris and Myles and Mylie and Alana and Tiffy and Timmy and Aunty Winter and Aunty Taryn and Aunty Tanya!" Tiffany rambled on in excitement.

"Yes, Aunty Tanya! She's soooo funny!" Timmy shouted and giggled at the same time.

"Yup, guys. We will be leaving on Friday to go see our family. But you still need to get to school and get through the next couple of days. So let's scidattle!"

The Unexpected

Taryn walked in the house, dropped her bags on the floor, and searched out a bag of M&M peanuts and a can of 7 Up. Alana went straight to her room and began her homework. Ryan stayed after school for cheerleading practice.

This was a long ass day! she thought to herself. *I should really consider Chase's offer. I'm exhausted dealing with some of the dysfunction these teachers are causing.* She sent the G-CODE. *I need to talk!*

The tension and frustration was evident in Taryn's voice. Her friends didn't like to hear her so upset. She began telling them about one of the teachers at her school.

"This chick just does not want to follow protocol. I'm all for creativity, but there are specific guidelines that we must adhere to. And she doesn't seem to get it! What she does or does not do impacts me as the leader of the school. I mean, I really like this young lady, and I want to help her develop, but she insists on doing things her way." Taryn let loose. The girls remained silent and gave Taryn her platform to vent.

"I had to tell her, 'Listen. I like you, and I want you to succeed, but you gotta follow the rules, or I will let your ass go!"

"Taryn!" Winter exclaimed in shock. "You didn't curse at her, did you?"

As if there were no other ways to approach it, Taryn responded, "Hell, yes, I did! I will let her ass go in a heartbeat." They all laughed.

"You are a mess!" Winter said.

Tanya changed the subject and led into her story. "Ummmmm . . ."

They all knew that whenever Tanya started off with an "ummm," there was a juicy story to follow. They were all ears.

"Y'all remember that guy I told you I met on my flight to LA two months ago?" She didn't give them a chance to answer and continued with her story. "Well, turns out he's the VP of marketing at Keiser Food Stores. I've been talking to him for the last few weeks. He's mad cool. He called me earlier this afternoon, letting me know he was in Houston on business and that his meeting ended early and wanted to know if I was available to meet him for lunch. I agreed to go since I was done scheduling my clients, packing for this weekend, and had the rest of the afternoon to myself.

"He sent a black car for me, and we met at Vic & Anthony's Steakhouse. The food and wine was soooo daggone good! Since he'd be in town overnight, he asked if I felt like hanging out a little longer. Of course, ya girl said yes because, babyyyy, 'peaches' was talking to me!"

They all burst into laughter. Tanya loved entertaining her besties with her tales of lust. She continued, "Girl, we got in that black car, and I *knew* what I was about to do. But I don't know if he *knew* what he was about to get into. Shitttttt! It actually turned out that I didn't know what the hell *I* was getting into my damn self! He told his driver to drive around for a bit while we figured out what we'd do next. I honestly can't remember what the hell he started talking about. All I know is I slid my hand into his pants and started rubbing his pulse. That shit was so freaking BIG! I did not expect that! I started caressing it and felt it getting harder and harder with each touch. Girl! I was so glad I had on a short sundress. He slid his pants down, slid a condom on, and pulled me on top of him. I started riding him slowly, only letting him halfway in. That was driving him crazy. He was grabbing my ass so tight and trying to slide me all the way down on his dick. That shit felt so good. I got a few scratches on my ass." She chuckled.

"I wanted to come so bad. Shit, I was *shocked* that I wanted to come so fast. But I'm telling you, that 'D' was so thick and long and smooth, it felt like velvet! He started begging me to "please" let him put it all the way in. I made his ass beg for about five minutes. Then I slid all the way down on him. Ooooh baby, all I could do was nibble on his ear. He sat me there for a minute, didn't let me move . . . like he just wanted to get familiar with his surroundings. Then he pumped up once, and I took over from there. I was sliding up and down and twirling my hips."

"He didn't know what to do. He grabbed my tits and started sucking on them so hard. I felt myself about to come, so I started riding him harder. He let out this sound, and I felt his shit pulsate, so I let loose. We came at the same damn time. That shit hasn't happened to me in so long! And before y'all chicks ask . . . the driver was right there . . . driving us around like he was told." She cracked up laughing, and her besties joined her.

"DAMN! Tanya, your freaky ass!" Mia said in between laughter. "I need to ride me some 'D'. Soon! My ass be so horny, I be wanting to snatch Toby right up in the elevator sometimes!" They all laughed.

"Girl, do it!" Tanya and Taryn said in unison.

"Yessss, bih! Do it!" Winter added. "'Cause you know, I'm gonna rock Charlie's brains out as soon as I get the opportunity." They all laughed.

"I love y'all, chicks. Y'all make a bad day feel like it never happened," Taryn added. "Well, let me go pay some bills so I'm not thinking about them while up there for the weekend. I'm *so* looking forward to seeing y'all heffas this weekend. We are gonna have a ball!"

They all said their goodbyes.

***

Taryn fed, bathed, and put Alana to bed. She made Ryan's plate, stuck it in the microwave, and crawled into her bed with her laptop to pay bills. Just as she finished paying her last bill, her phone buzzed.

CHASE: Hey, love! How was your day?

TARYN: It was so bad, babe. I'm so tired of this. I really am.

CHASE: Sorry to hear that, babe. Try not to think about it so much. I don't want you worrying ya pretty self.

TARYN: I'm not. Just got off the phone with the girls and their crazy asses. It took my mind off things.

TARYN: I miss you so much.

CHASE: Miss you too.

CHASE: lmao! my dudes told me I act like a bitch when I talk to you.

TARYN: LOL! Tell them shut up.

CHASE: It's all good you my baby.

TARYN: But yeah, babe. I'm so tired of this. I'm ready to just come out there.

CHASE: WORD! T, don't play with my head.

TARYN: Yes! I'm serious.

TARYN: I'm scared.

TARYN: You know the shit I been through. And I'm also a little afraid about starting my Charter School.

TARYN: Don't ever tell Mia I said that. She will kick my ass! With her go-getter behind. LOL

CHASE: Yeah, I know. But that's ya girl, and she knows you are the shit with the education thing.

TARYN: Yeah. She does luv her some me!

CHASE: So, Babe. What's ya plan? What u want me to do?

TARYN: Can you fly out here next week so we can talk it through?

CHASE: Yeah. I have a couple of meetings on Monday. But can catch a late flight. That's good for you?

TARYN: Yup. Thank you so much, babe. I really just need to see you.

CHASE: Anything for you, ma.

TARYN: OK. Let me hop in the shower and get these bags packed for the weekend. Sooo looking forward to seeing my chicks.

CHASE: OK. cool. Make sure you play with that thang and think about me.

CHASE: My dick is so hard right now just thinking about you in the shower.

TARYN. LOL...u r crazy, but I sure will.

CHASE: Will check on you later. Love you.

TARYN: Ditto.

What if I move and it doesn't work? Then I would have subjected Alana and Ryan to move from everything they know, and for nothing. I don't know. I'm too old to follow my heart. But I want this so bad. I know Chase loves me and the kids and would do anything for us and wouldn't do anything to hurt me. Ugh . . . why can't I just make a decision and go? Taryn pondered over the thought of moving to Las Vegas.

I know Winter would tell me to just step out on faith. I just gotta trust God. I'm just scared. She sighed and hopped in the shower.

This one is for you, Mr. Chase Durr. She smiled and began to please herself while romanticizing about her man.

Mia Gets A Drink

The day couldn't go by any faster for Mia. She was barely able to concentrate. Between all the e-mails, phone calls, people stopping by to congratulate her on her recent accomplishment and the anticipation of getting drinks with Toby after work, she scarcely got any work done. Toby passed by her office several times throughout the day to make sure she was OK. He knew how overwhelming it could be with everyone swarming around you and dropping a ton of e-mails to congratulate. He smiled each time he came by and witnessed someone handing Mia a card, giving her a hug, or simply saying congratulations.

All the sentiments were genuine as Mia was very well-liked around the firm, and everyone knew, especially Toby, just how much she deserved this honor. Her drive, tenacity, passion, and ambition were the things he adored about her; of course, her beautiful eyes, pretty smile, and knockout figure came in a very close second. Mia felt strangely safe and happy each time she noticed Toby come by.

Mia's phone buzzed at 4:32 p.m., just as she began packing her laptop into her black Saffiano leather crocodile Prada tote.

TOBY: Hey. Hope your day wasn't too overwhelming.

MIA: Hi Toby. It was, but in a good way.

TOBY: Would you like me to meet you in the lobby? The car will pick us up in front of the building.

MIA: Yes. That would be good. I just finished packing up my bag and am heading down now.

TOBY: OK. See you in a few minutes.

MIA: OK.

Mia felt anxious. *Why do I have butterflies? It's not like this is a date. But damn, I haven't felt like this in a very long time.* She shook off the thought and headed for the lobby. As she walked toward the front doors, she was greeted by Toby's warm smile and his arm extended to take her bag.

This damn man is fine as hell! She maintained her composure and handed the bag over to him. He opened the door and let her out. As she brushed past him, she smelled the scent of his cologne. At that moment, all she wanted to do was wrap her arms around his neck.

"The car is right there," Toby said, pointing to the dark Lincoln Black Label MKZ Hybrid. As she approached, the driver scurried around the car to open the door for her. Toby handed him their bags and slid in beside her. There was an awkward moment of silence until the driver got into the car.

The driver called out to Toby, "245 Eldridge Street?"

"Yup, you got it, Sam," Toby responded.

***

BAR GOTO? Never been here before. Very nice! I need to make a note for the next time Tanya is in town, Mia thought to herself as they walked inside the bar. Toby gestured for the bar as he grabbed two open seats at the end. He pulled out the bar stool for her to take a seat and then sat beside to her. She found the hook underneath the bar top and hung her purse on it.

Toby gestured for the bartender. "A bottle of champagne for the lady . . . Ace of Spades Brignac Brut." He turned to Mia. "Time to celebrate . . . PARTNER!" he said with a big genuine smile.

He is so freaking handsome and thoughtful, Mia couldn't help but think. "Thank you, Toby. And YES, time to CELEBRATE!" Mia responded enthusiastically.

They drank the entire bottle of champagne while they laughed about the latest office gossip and some of the events of the past year. In between stories and laughs, Mia found Toby staring at her. She pretended not to notice but consciously licked her lips and tilted her head just enough for him to have the best view of her from all angles.

"Would you like anything else to drink?" Toby asked Mia.

"Yes, pour it on!" She giggled. "I haven't had a real drink in months. Needed to be on my A-game at all times." She exclaimed,

"Well, another drink it is!"Toby gestured for the Bartender. "Another bottle! The lady of the day must get what she wants!"

The bartender smiled at Toby and Mia. "You guys make such a happy couple and are so super cute together," he said and headed off to grab their second bottle of champagne. They both glanced at each other and then quickly looked away, shocked at the assumption made by the bartender.

Couple? they were both thinking.

"You got that right. This is my girl!" Toby exclaimed, innocently and genuinely meaning that Mia was his good friend while secretly wishing she more than that.

As they finished up their last glass of champagne, Mia was in the mood to dance. The DJ was playing a mix of nineties hip-hop and R&B. Toby was enjoying the music and took pleasure in seeing Mia have such a good time. They hadn't realized it was nearly nine o'clock, and they'd been at the bar for over four hours.

As Toby was paying the check, the DJ slowed the music down. R. Kelly's *12 Play* bellowed through the speakers, and Mia instinctively got up to dance. This was one of her favorite songs. She grabbed Toby's hand and pulled him off his stool. Before either of them knew it, Mia wrapped her arms around his neck and rested her head on his shoulder, and he gently swathed his arms around her waist. They stood there. Still, for a moment. R. Kelly sang through the speakers.

One . . . we'll go to my room of fun . . .

Two . . . and I'll say give me your tongue . . .

Three . . . 'cause tonight I'm gonna fulfill your fantasies yeah . . .

Four . . ."

Mia and Toby slowly swayed back and forth, melting into each other's arms with each rock. She had not felt this cared for in a while. Toby soaked in the opportunity to be as close to the woman he found so beautiful and amazing. She felt a slight pulsating in her essence and almost jumped with embarrassment at the sensation.

I want this man so bad, she thought to herself as Toby was having his own similar thought.

"We should probably go," Mia said softly in his ear. Toby agreed, although he wished he could hold her in his arms forever.

Just as they got to the car, Mia gestured for the driver to hold off on opening the door. She turned to face Toby with a warm look of gratefulness on her face.

"Thank you so much, Toby. You have made this very special for me, and I truly appreciate all of your support, competition"—she chuckled and continued—"and encouragement."

Before he could respond, she leaned in and gently kissed him on his cheek and then once more right on his lips. Without hesitation, Toby immediately kissed her back. They embraced each other and indulged in a fervent kiss. Neither of them wanted to let go, and both consciously understood where this could lead. Mia stepped back a half inch, her waste still enveloped in his arms.

"I hope you don't think I'm a horrible person. I know Mor—"

He put his finger to her lips before she could finish her statement. "Mia, I could never think you're a horrible person. You are the most caring, good-natured, and beautiful woman I know. Whatever your reasons are, I'm sure they are good, and you have done all you can before getting to this point. So please, no need to feel bad or apologize. I'm just happy that you are here with me."

She smiled, leaned in, and softly kissed him again.

"I better get you home," Toby whispered and opened the car door for her to get in.

Before stepping in, she turned back to him and said, "I'm not ready to go home."

Toby was pleasantly surprised and smiled., He didn't hesitate to call out to the driver, "525 Park Avenue." He turned to Mia. "Are you sure?"

She shook her head, eyes locked with his, and said "Yes." They held hands with fingers intertwined the entire ride to Toby's Park Avenue penthouse.

***

The first thing Mia noticed when they walked in was how immaculate and big Toby's place was. She also noticed that there was a huge ebony-colored satin Steinway piano in the far corner of his living room.

"You play?" she asked, pointing at the piano.

"Yes. It's something I do in my spare time and as a stress reliever. My great-grandfather, grandfather, and dad played. So, the passion has been passed down through generations," he proudly responded.

"May I hear something?" she shyly asked.

Without hesitating, he dropped his blazer on the brown leather tufted sofa, hit a button on the wall, which turned on the brick-lined fireplace, and headed over to the piano. He began to play a tune familiar to her ears; Freddie Jackson's, "You Are My Lady" strummed through the space of the room. He played beautifully. Mia walked over, sat beside him, placed her head on his shoulder and listened to him play for a while. As the song was nearing its end, she placed her hand on his cheek and turned his face toward hers.

"Thank you," she softly whispered and leaned in to kiss him. As he stood, he grabbed her by the hand to stand with him. They were locked in a passionate kiss, and he blindly guided her toward his bathroom. She stepped out of her heels one by one as he slid her skirt down her legs, followed by her thong. Then he slithered her blazer off and slowly released one button at a time on her blouse. Mia returned the favor and unbuttoned his shirt, exposing his muscular chest and abs. She then unlatched his pants and slid them down with boxer briefs in tow. With a quick motion he turned her around and leaned her over the stainless-steel marble-top sink and glided himself into her from behind while loosening her bra and allowing it to fall off her shoulders.

Mia perked her ass high enough so that every ounce of him was inside of her. He stroked slow and hard, each time allowing himself to feel her complete warmth around him. She relished each stroke and the fullness of him inside of her. Just as he was succumbing to his ecstasy, Mia felt a jolt inside of herself. She held on to the rim of the sink and enjoyed the explosion.

Take Off

"I'm just scared!" Taryn exclaimed to Tanya as she held the phone to her ear with her shoulder while helping Alana into the black car waiting to transport them to the airport.

"I know you are. But you were the one who told *me* to step out on faith and start build *my own* clientele instead of working for a designer. I was nervous, but look at me now, I'm styling, designing, and making moves. Why? Because I listened to you and stayed true to my dreams", Tanya reminded her best friend. "It's time you take a step out on faith. Go be with your man. He loves you! And start that charter school. Taryn, you can do this!"

Taryn knew deep down in her heart that Tanya was right. While her fear was rational, she knew she couldn't live the rest of her life afraid to take chances.

"I know," she said with a sigh.

"OK, girlie. We'll talk about it some more this weekend since we'll all be together. Let me get to the airport. Love you and see you in a few. It's about to go DOWN!"

They laughed in agreement.

***

"Come on, guys! We gotta get to the airport. Grab your bags, and let's scidattle!" Winter yelled out to the twins.

They both came running into the garage, luggage in tow. Winter packed the bags into the trunk of her jet-black Cadillac CTS with Morello Red accents. She blasted their favorite "Kidz Bop" tunes and bopped her head along with the kids as they sang every song that came bellowing through the speakers. They arrived at the airport, parked, and headed for their terminal. The twins were beaming with excitement about seeing their aunts and cousins. They also knew Uncle Morris would have something special for them to do as he always did, and they couldn't wait to find out what that would be.

"Mom how come you, Auntie Mia, Auntie Tanya, and Auntie Taryn are staying at a hotel?" TJ inquisitively asked.

"This is a special weekend for your auntie Mia, and we have planned some fun activities for the grown-ups this weekend, and part of that is us having a sleepover at the hotel. Kinda like what you do with your friends for special occasions," Winter explained.

"Oh. OK. Makes sense to me," TJ responded as if he were giving her his permission. She smiled. TJ didn't shy away from the fact that he was now the "man" of the house.

"OK, guys, off we go!" Winter announced as they departed for New York City.

***

Tanya packed her bag and hopped in the car to head to the airport. Her phone rang. It was Jemarious.

"Hello, Ms. Mack. How are you today?"

"Hello, Jemarious. I'm doing well. Heading to the airport to catch my flight to NYC," she responded, slightly curious about the reason for his call.

"Yeah. I remember you mentioning that you'd be in NYC for the weekend. Actually, that's why I am calling. Wanted to see if you and your girls would be interested in coming out Saturday night to Rose Bar? My homie is DJing on Saturday, and he is dat dude wit' old school hip-hop. I know you and your girls love old school, so y'all can be my guests," he offered.

"Oh yeah. Mia would love that! Let me check with the girls when I get to NYC, and I will let you know for sure."

Jemarious was a little surprised that she even considered but was happy she did. He thought she was cool and wanted to get an opportunity to be around her on *nonbusiness.*

"OK. Cool. Hit me back. Have a safe flight, Ms. Mack."

***

Mia pranced around her office all morning, excited to see her besties, nieces, and nephew. She also couldn't stop thinking about the night before with Toby.

OMG. Wait until I tell the girls! They are going to be so happy! Her mind darted to Morris, and she quickly shrugged it off. *I hate that it had to come to this. But we haven't been intimate in nearly two years. And besides, who am I kidding? Our marriage is over. It's not like I don't know about his little "secret." We are good friends and good parents and have stayed together for the kids.*

Mia hated that this was what had become of their marriage. But both she and Morris knew that as long as Mia maintained her career, there wasn't any hope for them.

Pathetic. I'll never understand why my having a career is so hard for him to accept. And damn! He hasn't even expressed one ounce of congratulations for me making partner. Mia's good mood almost drifted away, but she quickly caught herself.

Enough about Morris. She sat in her chair and allowed her mind to replay the events of the night before. She smiled at how warm her heart felt as she recalled Toby washing her body from head to toe in the shower and kissing her along the way. He was so sensual and attentive. He reminded her over and over about how much he wished she were all his, how happy he'd be, and how hard he'd work to make sure she was just as happy. She was awaken from her daydream at the sound of tapping on her office door. She thought it was Frances since everyone else is usually announced.

"Yes. Come in, Frances," she welcomingly called out.

Peeking his head through the door as he slowly opened it, Toby confessed, "No. It's not Frances. I convinced her to let me in without being announced."

Mia smiled and waved him in. Toby closed the door behind himself and walked towards her. She stood up from her chair and met him along the way. They immediately embraced and shared a quick peck on the lips.

"Hey there!" Toby greeted her.

"Hey, you," she said back. They stood there for a moment, taking in each other's presence in.

Toby broke the silence. "Excited to see your girls tonight?"

Mia lit up at the thought. “I can’t wait! We haven’t had a weekend like this in over a year,” she continued to beam. “Aren’t you coming to the Carnegie Bar later? I would love for you to meet them.”

Toby smiled. He was excited for Mia and was looking forward to meeting her friends. “I will be there for sure. Just wanted to stop by and say hello. I know you’re a busy woman these days, being partner and all,” he said with a wry smile.

Mia laughed and said, “Yes! Isn’t there some work you need to attend to yourself?”

They both laughed. He gave her a quick peck on the cheek and exited her office. Mia took in a deep breath. Being with Toby made her feel so good. The day couldn’t go by fast enough. She needed to see her girls.

Taryn Commits

It was the perfect beginning to an amazing weekend for Taryn. As she and Alana were heading toward the exit after picking up their luggage from the baggage carousel, she noticed a man in an all-black suit standing at the door, holding up a card with, "Ms. TARYN JACKSON" scribed on it. She was a bit surprised as she didn't recall scheduling a car service to pick them up from the airport. She shrugged it off and assumed that perhaps Mia sent a car for them. *After all, she is such a gracious host,* Taryn thought to herself.

The driver guided them toward his black Lincoln Town Car and opened the door for them. Sitting there, with a big grin on his face, was Chase. Taryn was taken by surprise, screamed with excitement, and asked, "What are you doing here?"

Chase responded, "Had to see my girls!"

Alana was so excited, she jumped in the car, wrapped her arms around his neck, and planted a big kiss on his cheek. "Mr. Chase! Where did you come from?" she asked excitedly.

Taryn loved to see how much Alana and Ryan liked and enjoyed being around Chase. She climbed in the car behind Alana while the driver loaded their luggage in the trunk. She leaned over and gave him a quick peck on his lips. "What are you doing here? Not that I'm not completely happy to see you, babe. But I thought you had some business to take care of this weekend." She couldn't help but smile while inquiring. After all, she was thrilled to see her man.

"I do have some business to take care of this weekend. I'm flying back out west later this evening. But since I was here yesterday, I decided to stay over so that I could see you and give you this in person." He pulled out an American Express Black Card with her name imprinted on it and handed it over to her. "Show Mia and the girls a wonderful time this weekend. Get whatever you want."

Taryn was entirely astounded and didn't know what to say. All she could muster up was a sarcastic remark, "It better not be counterfeit!" and laughed. "No, but seriously . . . thank you, babe. I really appreciate it."

They smiled at each other as the car drove through the maze of Manhattan's traffic.

Chase broke the silence. "Where y'all staying this weekend?"

Taryn lit up again at the thought of spending the weekend with her besties. "Mandarin Oriental. None of us have stayed there before, but one of Tanya's clients recommended it to her. They said a suite would fit the four of us nicely since we were adamant about all staying in the same room. And the views are supposed to be really nice."

Chase smiled. He loved seeing Taryn happy and being able to make that happen for her. "Well, the room is on me!"

Taryn smiled and shook her head. *He spoils me so much!*

"Mr. Chase, you spoil my mom!" Alana blurted out. They all laughed.

After checking into the hotel, Chase and the driver escorted Taryn and Alana to Mia's place. The car pulled up in front of her Central Park West condo, Chase hopped out and opened the door for them while the driver pulled Alana's bag out of the trunk. As the doorman came over to assist with taking the bag into the building, Alana gave Chase another big hug.

"See ya, Mr. Chase!" she said and ran into the lobby behind the doorman.

Taryn faced Chase. "You are too good to me," she said and kissed him on his cheek.

"Nah! You too good to me. As much shit as these dudes put you through, you still standing and you still found it in ya heart to mess with a dude like me. I'll never make you regret that, and I will always do the shit that will keep a smile on ya face, ma!" He smacked her ass and continued, "And I will lay it down *often!*"

They both burst into laughter. "Yeah! You better!" Taryn agreed.

"You are crazy!" he jokingly replied.

"But you love it!" Taryn said, smiling.

He grabbed her hand, kissed her on her forehead, and softly said, "More than you'll ever know."

Before she had a second to gather her thoughts, she blurted out, "We're moving to Vegas!" Stunned at herself, she just stood there, not sure what to do or say next. Chase was just as surprised.

"Really, babe? Don't fuck wit' my head!"

She nodded. Chase grabbed her by the waist and pulled her in close to him, laying kisses all over her face. "Go! Have a great weekend wit' ya girls. I will be at the house when you get home, so we can plan this shit out . . . *before* you change ya crazy ass mind."

They laughed. Taryn gave him a peck on the lips, turned, and headed into the lobby.

Weekend let's get it!

Reunion

Taryn knocked on the door of Mia's duplex, penthouse, twenty-eight floors elevated in the sky. *My girl is the shit,* she acknowledged while she waited for someone to answer the door. She was sure the nanny would come to the door, but to her pleasant surprise, it was Winter. Taryn dropped her Kate Spade tote and screamed, "Heyyyyyyyy, bitchhhhhh! OMG, Winter! I love you! I miss you!", while hugging her best friend.

"What's up, girl? I love you. I miss you too!" Winter embraced her and screamed back.

Alana looked on in amusement. She loved seeing her mom so happy. TJ and Tiffany ran to Alana, jumping all over her, "Alana! Alana! Alana!" they sang out. Alana hugged her cousins, laughing and greeting them back. Then they all swapped; the twins were on Taryn's thighs, and Alana was in Winter's arms. The nanny watched the interaction with pleasure and greeted Taryn and Alana while grabbing their bags from the front door.

"Mrs. Mia and the kids will be here shortly. She told me to tell you all to make yourselves at home," Louisa, the nanny, warmly announced. The kids ran off to the game room Morris had set up for Myles and Mylie, while Taryn and Winter sat on the sofa in the main living room, catching up. About thirty minutes later, the front door opened as Mia, Mylie, and Myles entered the penthouse.

"Aunties!" Mylie yelled out and ran to embrace Taryn and Winter. Myles swiftly walked over, trying to maintain his 'coolness' and hugged his aunts.

"Myles, you are getting so big!" Winter assured him. He smiled, loving this acknowledgment. Simultaneously, Mia dropped her Jackie O' Gucci bag and ran over to her besties. They met her halfway and embraced in a three-way hug.

"Mia! OMG! Mia! I'm so proud of you. So happy to see you. I love you. OMG! You made it!" Taryn screamed with tears of joy in her eyes.

"Yessss, Mia! I'm so proud of you! I love you!" Winter added.

Mia thanked her besties over and over, "Thank you, thank you, thank you! I miss y'all soooo much. I'm so happy y'all are here!" she exclaimed as her eyes welled up with tears. The three ladies all allowed tears to stroll down their faces while smiling and embracing.

Myles and Mylie ran off to the game room as they heard their cousins laughing and oohing over the games. Just as they had been loud with excitement, the ladies heard the kids scream out with joy as they all greeted Myles and Mylie.

Just then, the doorbell rang, and Louisa looked toward Mia who shrugged as she wasn't expecting anyone else since Tanya told them she'd meet them at the hotel. Louisa answered the door to find Tanya in the doorway.

Tanya walked in, announcing herself, "It's me, bitches!"

Mia, Winter, and Taryn all shouted, "Tanyaaaaaa!" and ran over to embrace her.

Tanya yelled, "My chicks! My chiiiicccckssssssss! I miss y'all! I love y'all! OMG, Mia. Congratulations, girl! You did it! I knew you would!"

The ladies were locked in arms as they walked over to the sofa. "Tanya, I thought you were going to meet us at the hotel?" Winter asked.

"I was, but you know I could not miss a chance to see my babies . . . I need to see my nieces and nephews," she responded. "Where are they?"

Mia pointed toward the back, the direction of the game room. "Wait, I'm going back there too. I need to see my nieces and nephew as well." Mia added.

Tanya grabbed a bag of goodies she'd brought with her, and they headed towards the game room. The kids were excited to see both Mia and Tanya; the yells and screams confirmed that.

"Auntie Tanya! Auntie Mia!" the kids greeted. Winter and Taryn could hear them at the front of the penthouse. Louisa smiled to herself and appreciated all the love displayed among the group.

Cigar Bar

Mia, Winter, and Tanya grabbed their bags, and they all headed down to the black car waiting to take them to the hotel. Taryn had dropped her bags off earlier and got them checked into their suite. Mia's cell rang. She quickly answered. It was Frances.

"Hey, Fran. Everything OK?" she asked.

"Yup! Just wanted to make sure you're all set to be at the Carnegie Bar by 7:00 p.m. for dinner. The managing partners and rest of the office team will all be arriving at that time. Dinner will be from seven to nine, and then Mr. Dodson has reserved a cigar room for everyone for cocktails and cigars." Frances ran down the evening plans. "Oh! And Toby was able to get the owner to agree to serve a full dinner instead of the normal light fare they usually offer and to have the music of your choice played in the cigar room. He hooked you up!" She chuckled, secretly knowing how much Toby cared for Mia.

"Confirmed, Fran! Thank you and looking forward to seeing you later. You finally get to meet the girls!" Mia giggled.

***

Dinner was great. The Ladies enjoyed the company of Mia's boss and colleagues. They loved Frances; she made herself right at home with them. They especially enjoyed watching Toby check Mia out throughout dinner. He couldn't keep his eyes off her. He was very attentive to her enjoyment, ensuring she never ran low on her Grey Goose shaken with cranberry and iced water with lemon. Mia glowed around him. She was happy, and her friends knew it. As dinner was wrapping up, Tanya's phone rang. She excused herself to answer when she identified that it was Jemarious.

"Hello. Ms. Mack here," she answered in the most professional voice she could muster up, trying to hide the slur of her tongue from the three glasses of Hennessey she'd just downed.

"Hi, Ms. Mack. It's JR. Sorry to bother you while you're at dinner. Just wanted to see, since I'm in town, if you'd be OK with me stopping by the cigar bar to chill with you and your people. If not, it's OK. Just thought I'd ask."

Stop by and chill? Does he realize he's my client, not my homeboy? BUT I truly wouldn't mind him coming through. I'm sure Mia's colleagues would get a kick out of having an NBA player join us for cigars, she thought to herself.

"Sure. I'm sure it'll be OK with Mia and the girls."

"Okay, cool. I'll be there around nine forty-five," he confirmed before hanging up. Just as Tanya was getting back to the table, the group was preparing to head to the reserved cigar room. She quickly walked over and whispered in Mia's ear, "Jemarious is going to stop by. And before you ask, yes, bih, my new client."

They both chuckled.

"OK. Cool with me," Mia accepted.

***

Toby grabbed a seat for Mia and the girls. Mia's boss, Mr. Dodson, walked over to them, opened a cherry oakwood cigar box, and presented it for each of them to grab one.

"These are the best! And, Mia, you certainly deserve the best!" he exclaimed. They each took a cigar, and he offered to cut and light for them.

"Ladies, I am so very proud of your friend here. She is the toughest person I know. She don't take no shit. When she wants a deal, she gets her deal. I have the utmost respect for her."

Just as he was giving his honest yet drunken speech, the waitress graciously interrupted and handed them all a glass of whiskey.

"A toast to Mia, our new partner and respected friend! Well deserved!"

Everyone held up their glasses in salute. Just then, the music began flowing through hidden speakers.

What y'all know about a supermodel
Fresh out of Elle magazine
Buy her own bottles
Look, pimp juice, I need me one
Bad than a mother

I hear you sayin' I need a bad girl
If you're a bad girl

They bopped their heads to Usher in agreement; they were some "bad" girls.

Toby grabbed Mia by the hand and escorted her to the middle of the room. They began dancing and two-stepping. Taryn was surprised to see how much rhythm Toby moved with. She leaned over and whispered to Winter, "You sure he ain't got no black in him."

Winter burst into laughter. She and Taryn got up and joined them in the middle of the makeshift dance floor, along with Mr. Dodson and a host of the other guests. The music was flowing nicely and kept everyone out of their seats and committed to the dance floor. Even Frances and Mr. Dodson were bopping together and enjoying each other's company.

***

Jemarious was escorted into the room by the hostess. Tanya walked over to greet him and tilted her head for him to follow her toward Mia. She tapped Toby on the shoulder to make her presence known and then proceeded to introduce Jemarious to both him and Mia.

"JR, this is my girl, Mia. Mia, this is Jemarious Russell." He stretched out his hand to shake hers and congratulated her on making partner. Tanya then turned and introduced Toby. "JR, this is Tobias, Mia's"—she hesitated a little as she almost introduced him as 'Mia's man'—"Mia's colleague."

They both stretched out their hands and greeted each other. "Great game the other night! Hope the shoulder is OK," Toby said, acknowledging that he knew who he was.

"Thanks! Still a little sore, but nothing I can't play through."

Mia and Toby returned to their two-step, while Tanya led JR over to meet Winter and Taryn. They were stopped a few times as they walked over. JR shook a few hands and thanked those who gave him compliments on his games. Mr. Dodson offered him a cigar and drink and alerted the waiter to allow JR to make his selection. After introducing JR to her friends, they headed over to a corner seat, puffed on their cigars, and sipped their whiskey.

"Well, Mr. Russell, you have my attention. What are you really doing here?" Tanya curiously asked.

"You look stunning, Ms. Mack . . . simply gorgeous," he replied. "I'm here to enjoy your company. I thought you were cool from the moment I met you. Just wanted to hang out."

Tanya was flattered. "Thank you, Mr. Russell. But I know you did not come all this way to pay me no compliment."

JR laughed. He loved how straightforward and down-to-earth Tanya was. This was what he found to be so refreshing about her. She was different from the usual stuck-up "I'm too cute, and my clothes are too nice to have fun" women, or those "I'll do and be whatever you want me to be, just so I can be in the face of an NBA player" groupie women he regularly encountered. Tanya could care less about his stature or fame. She was confident in herself and was a damn good stylist. She also had that hood swag and could switch up from an articulate professional to a slang-talking OG. Her best friends complemented her swag as they all carried the same demeanor.

"I hope you don't mind me being so forward. But I have not stopped thinking about you since we met. Each time we talk, I don't want to hang up. I even find myself finding reasons to call you. You are so different than these other women, and it makes me want to be around you more."

Tanya was a little caught off guard, yet flattered. "JR, I am flattered. However, I don't mix business with pleasure. I've seen things get messy in my line of business. And this is my livelihood. I *will not* mess up my money."

JR understood how messy things could get when mixing business with pleasure. He also had a standard not to do so. However, Tanya was different, and she made him want to take a different perspective, of course, only if he were to be with her.

"Ms. Mack . . . it would be my pleasure to give you the business," he smoothly responded with a smile on his face. "But I would first like to spend some time getting to know you better. All I'm asking is that you think about it. Let's enjoy tonight and tomorrow if you all decide to come through." She agreed.

The music was great. Tanya and JR joined the rest of the party on the dance floor. They all danced, drank, and enjoyed the evening. Everyone, including Mr. Dodson and Frances, the two eldest of the bunch, stayed until closing.

***

Toby walked them to their black car, ensuring they were OK, and that the driver knew their destination. As they loaded into the car, they each warmly thanked him and gave him a, "Thanks for taking care of my girl", look.

Mia turned to him before getting in the car and planted a kiss right on his lips. He was surprised, but kissed her back... with one eye open, checking to see if her friends bore witness. They all pretended not to notice, looking down at their cell phones as if whatever was on the screen were more important than seeing their best friend kiss this man. She melted into her seat, and he closed the door behind her.

"GIRLLLLLLLL!" Taryn exaggerated the word. "What the fudge? Did I just see you kiss Toby?"

She, Winter, and Tanya burst into curious laughter. Mia sat there with a huge Cheshire-cat smile on her face.

"I guess I should tell y'all now instead of waiting until we get to the hotel," she began to confess.

"Bitch! Tell us what? Yes, tell us now!" Taryn commanded with excitement, already anticipating what she was about to hear.

"Yes, chick, let it out! Right here," Tanya urged.

"Yesssss . . . I need to hear this now!" Winter added to the sense urgency in hearing what Mia had to tell them.

Mia threw her head back and laughed. "Guess I'll tell y'all chicks now since y'all can't wait until we get to the hotel." Mia proceeded with giving them the details of the night before. She vividly recalled every moment spent with Toby—from drinking and dancing in the bar, his playing Freddie Jackson's "You Are My Lady" on his piano, him being inside of her in his bathroom, to sharing a sensual and romantic hot shower together. She reminisced over the sultry way he washed her body from head to toe and the gentle way he tasted her love. They all sat there in amazement.

"Miaaaaaa . . ." Winter broke the silence. "Girl, that sounds amazing, romantic, *and* slutty!" They all laughed. "But I am so happy for you. You deserve a good and attentive man. And that man is certainly crazy about you. I won't mess up the mood and ask about Morris. We can talk about that ninja tomorrow." Winter chuckled and rolled her eyes.

"Yassss, bitch! It's about damn time! If you didn't do it by now, I was planning on asking Toby, what the fuck is up." They laughed out loud again at Taryn's directness.

"Mia, listen. I know you well. I know this wasn't a fly-by-night decision. You must really have feelings for Toby and must be equally done with Morris. We understand. It took longer than we all probably thought it would, but I'm so glad you are moving on. You and Morris have developed a great friendship and are good parents, but we know that's about all it will ever be with Morris if you continue to pursue your career aspirations. We'll never understand his mind-set. But at this point, who gives a rat's ass? As long as you find someone who makes you happy, celebrates you, and appreciates you . . . And, girl, it ain't hard to tell that's Toby. Ummm . . . and he got some good 'D'! Ooooh, babyyyy!" There was more laughter and nods of agreement on the wisdom Tanya shared.

Hotel

As they entered the suite, they noticed a basket full of wine, chocolates, and other goodies and a full bouquet of long-stem white roses sitting on the console. Each had a small card attached. The goodie basket was addressed to Mia and read, *"Congratulations. Love, Your Bro, Chase."* The bouquet was for Taryn; the card read, *"Have a great weekend, babe. Love you."*

Mia looked at Taryn as she read her card and said, "Girl, that man loves you and is doing his best to show you. Don't penalize him for Ron's dumb ass."

Taryn knew Mia was right. She announced to her girls, "I'm gonna do it! We're going to move to Vegas." They were all happy and very supportive of her decision.

"Well . . . more to celebrate this weekend!" Mia announced, grabbing a bottle of wine from the basket while Winter pulled out four glasses from the cabinet. She poured each a glass, and they toasted to new loves and new beginnings.

It felt like their teenage years when they would all sleep over Taryn's grandparent's house in Chicago. They snacked, drank two more bottles of wine, and chatted until 5:00 a.m. Taryn dozed in and out as usual, jumping into the conversation with sarcasm, a curse, or a joke before nodding back off. They hadn't laughed so hard in a long time.

Tanya teased Taryn, "We need to get this chick checked into a sleep clinic for a sleep study. She falls asleep midsentence and then wakes up saying some silly or sarcastic shit."

They all burst into laughter and shared stories of times where Taryn fell asleep—in a club in Miami, during dinner at Bandera's in Chicago for her very own birthday, and at church one Easter Sunday.

"She's narcoleptic," Winter teased.

"Well, let's at least try and get a few hours of sleep. We got the spa at 10:00 a.m." Mia stretched and headed for the room to change into the pj's supplied to them all by Tanya.

Versace pj's? Only my girl Tanya. She smiled with gratefulness. They all followed and turned in for a few hours of sleep.

Tanya's phone buzzed—a voice mail. She didn't realize she missed her phone ring. She quickly checked her message; it was from JR.

∞

"Hey, pretty lady. Hope you enjoyed your evening. It was good seeing you. Think about what I said . . . Good night."

∞

She smiled at the phone and then rolled her eyes. *Too bad I don't mix business with pleasure.*

Big Spender

At 8:30 a.m., Winter opened her eyes to the smell of coffee, eggs, turkey bacon, and toast. She walked into the kitchen and found Mia pouring coffee for them all. Mia had always been an early riser, no matter what time she went to bed the night before. She was dressed in her workout clothes and had small beads of sweat sitting on her forehead.

"Morning, sunshine!" she greeted Winter. "Stopped and grabbed a light breakfast after taking a quick morning run. Gonna hop in the shower and get ready for the spa at ten. I can't wait for some tranquility."

Taryn and Tanya both dragged themselves out of bed and into the kitchen for their morning cup of Joe.

"Mia, why yo' ass always gotta pop up out of bed all early every damn morning? *But* I am so thankful you do. Otherwise, I'd be grumpy from not having breakfast or my coffee." They all laughed at Taryn's coupled complaint and compliment. Mia hurried them to eat and shower so that they wouldn't be late for their spa appointments.

***

"That was sooooo relaxing," Winter wooed about the spa. "Mia, thank you for choosing the calm-mind retreat package for me. I desperately needed that."

"Yes, you selected the perfect package for each of us. I love it!" Tanya chimed in. "Now, ladies, let's throw something on and get on our way. I have a surprise for you all."

Tanya threw on a black Chanel velour sweat suit, some black Chanel sneakers, and her signature oversized black Celine butterfly sunglasses. Mia got ready in some black Alexander McQueen mesh leggings, a pair of black Alexander McQueen hobnail metal toe-cap boots, black Banana Republic T-shirt, oversized black Alexander McQueen knitted bomber jacket, and her oversized Gucci oval sunglasses. Winter adorned herself in an oversized black silk MiH knee-length shirtdress, a pair of black leather Chanel espadrilles, and her smoke-black Quay Australia Kitty sunglasses. Taryn joined the crowd, doused in her black ripped Donna Karan slim-fit jeans, black cotton Style Parinde round-neck

T-shirt, black pebbled Tory Burch Reva flats, and her favorite black Gucci square sunglasses.

These women set their own rules on fashion and enjoyed adorning themselves in sleek styles which expressed their self-confidence, highlighted their enticing curves and individual identities. Even on a dress-down day, they stepped out in style, and anyone who knew them knew this to be their truth. They grabbed their bags and headed out the door, all eager to find out what surprise Tanya had cooked up.

"Owwwww, my bitches! *All black* eeerrrthang!" Tanya teased. They all exploded with laughter.

***

They walked into the Gucci store on 5th Avenue, and Tanya and promptly said, "Let me go talk to Sheila and see if my package has arrived. I preordered some stuff for us."

They were all still wearing their shades; the night before they drank and partied like it was 1999 and then stayed up chatting into the early morning at the hotel. They felt great just being together. The love they shared for one another was like that of biological sisters. Aside from Mia who has an older brother, none of them had any siblings.

They caroused the store while they waited for Tanya. Mia picked up a black briefcase with nickel hardware. "I think I'm going to buy this for myself as a celebratory gift."

Taryn swiftly grabbed the briefcase from her and handed it to the associate. "Ring that up for my girl." With a huge smile on her face, she turned to Mia and said, "It's on me."

Mia smiled back in appreciation of her friend's kind gesture. "THANK YOU, TARYN!" she exclaimed and gave her a big bear hug. Tanya walked back on the show floor, with Sheila toting a huge box, singing, *"So you wanna be a baller, shot caller, brawler . . ."*

The girls started two-stepping and laughing. Tanya was excited that the goodies she'd preordered had arrived in time for their weekend. Sheila sat the box down, and Tanya dug right in. She had an enormous smile on her face; she loved surprising her besties. She pulled out the first gift.

"Winter, my love. This is for you," she said, handing Winter a cubed box. Winter ripped into the box and let out a yelp upon seeing the silver G-Timeless watch.

"Tanya, thank you, babes!" She put her watch on and started modeling her wrist for Taryn and Mia.

Next, Tanya handed Taryn a thin square box. Taryn was so eager to open her gift that she dropped the box on the floor. "Oh shit! Ooopps . . . pardon me," she excused herself. They all laughed.

"Slow down, chick!" Tanya scolded her and laughed again. Taryn opened her box and tilted her head to the side, feeling warmth and love for the beautiful silver interlocking G bracelet she'd just unveiled.

"Awe, poo, thank you. This is beautiful," she said with sincere appreciation. Tanya then turned to Mia and handed her a small cubed box and two shoe-sized boxes.

"Mia, my love, my friend, my sister. My mom and I are so proud of you. Ever since we were little girls, she knew you'd be a boss bitch. I knew you'd just be bossy!" Both she and Mia burst out laughing, and Mia's eyes welled with tears. Tanya continued, "Nah, just kidding. I knew you'd be great at whatever you set your mind to. I have so much respect for you and am proud to call you my friend. Thank you for always having my best interest at heart . . . and getting on my nerves about always leaving NYC . . . and, most of all, for looking after my mom while I'm away."

At this point, they were all crying. Mia conjured up enough clarity to speak through her tears. "Tanya, thank you so much! Thank all of you! I love you, ladies, and I truly appreciate all of your support and the gifts, but mostly, our sisterhood." They embraced in a group hug.

Taryn broke the ice. "OK, chicks! Let's get going to lunch. I'm starving. And I want me a good, *good* burger from Jackson Hole."

Before leaving, Tanya picked up a burgundy patent leather clutch with matching peep-toe booties. As she lusted over the combination, she found herself boasting, "Yeah . . . Jackson will love this!"

Time stood still for a minute. They all turned and look at her in shock. She had a look of embarrassment on her face and pretended she didn't notice their eyes piercing at her.

Almost in unison, they exclaimed, "Jackson?" She tried to ignore them and continued making her purchase.

"When are you planning on seeing Jackson?" Winter asked. Tanya hesitated to answer, knowing her friends would disapprove of any contact and communication with the man she was supposed to despise.

"He will be in Houston in a few weeks and asked if we could meet up for dinner while he's in town. Nothing more, nothing less." Tanya nonchalantly replied.

Just as Winter was about to reel in on the matter, Tanya was saved by the bell; Sheila asked them all if they were satisfied with their inventory and whether she could help with anything else. Both Mia and Taryn shook their heads and replied, "No, thank you." Tanya thanked Sheila and notified her that she'd be back in a couple of weeks with her new client.

Winter, not intending to be rude, did not provide a response to Sheila. She was fuming at the thought of Tanya seeing Jackson. They all hated Jackson for the drama he caused Tanya in college, the damage he almost did to her career, and the ultimate disrespect he displayed toward her and Winter during a visit at Winter's bed-and-breakfast a few years earlier where he had the nerve to show up with another woman for the weekend.

As they walked out of the store, Winter turned to Tanya and began to drill her with questions about Jackson. Knowing this could take a wrong turn, Mia intercepted, "Let's not do this now, y'all. Let's enjoy the weekend and our time together. Jackson has ruined enough lives as it is. Let's not let his bullshit ruin our weekend. But T, we certainly *will* get back to this at some point. This Jackson mess cannot happen again."

No one objected to Mia's request to leave the topic alone for now. They switched gears back to the fun and purpose of their weekend.

"Can we get that burger now?" Taryn asked. They all burst into laughter.

Saturday Night Shenanigans

Said, "Lil ——,
you can't —— with me if you wanted to"
These expensive, these is red bottoms,
these is bloody shoes
Hit the store, I can get 'em both
I don't wanna . . .

The rhythmic lyrics of Cardi B's, "Bodak Yellow" blasted through the speakers of the black car. As they were bopping in their seats, Mia's cell phone rang. She looked at the caller ID and rolled her eyes when she saw Morris's name pop up.

He couldn't . . . or didn't want to make dinner and cigars on Friday. I haven't heard from him all day today. What could he possibly be calling me for right now? Mia thought to herself. She signaled for the driver to turn down the music as she answered the phone.

"Hey," she said dryly.

"Hey. Just calling to let y'all know I'm taking the kids out to dinner tonight. We'll be out pretty late since I just got here at eight. I also wanted to confirm that none of the kids have any seafood allergies," he informed and inquired with her.

"Nope. No allergies to seafood for any of them," she confirmed.

"OK. Good. Have fun. See you when you get back to *your* kids," he sarcastically said.

Mia rolled her eyes. *MY kids? He's being such an asshole. I don't understand why he acts like I'm only defined by my children. But I'm not going to let Morris's ass mess up my weekend.* "OK. Bye." She quickly ended the call.

"I think I need to hear some Lil' Kim. ...Get Money..." she rapped and bopped her head.

"Ohhhhh shit! Let's get it, bihhhhh!" Taryn shouted. They all laughed out loud. The music flowed as they made their way to the party Jemarious invited them to.

***

As they walked up to the bouncer at the door, Tanya announced that they were guests of Jemarious Russell. He quickly checked a list he pulled from his back pocket and directed them to enter. The DJ was playing a medley of old school hip-hop tunes as they made their way to the VIP section. Jemarious spotted them as they walked across the room.

Damn! Tanya is a dime. Her girls are fire too. Just then, he and Tanya caught eyes, and a bright smile crossed his face. Tanya played cool, although she was beaming on the inside.

He's your client. Remember that, T! she reminded herself. Jemarious reached out to hug her as she stepped into the entrance of the reserved section. She reciprocated his embrace, taking in a quick sniff of his Tom Ford cologne. *He smells so damn good!* She smiled and proceeded to an open seat on the leather tufted bench. He greeted each of them with a quick hug.

"Glad y'all could make it." He stopped at Mia, thanked her for coming, and congratulated her again on making partner. He then handed a small gift box to her. She was shocked at the gesture but certainly appreciative.

What a way to try and impress Tanya! she thought to herself and gave him a warm smile and then whispered in his ear, "Nice way to impress my girl," and winked at him. He couldn't help but smile.

Jemarious was a gracious host. He made sure they had bottles of champagne flowing all night. There were appetizers, and the waitresses were there, ensuring they had water, napkins, and utensils. While they weren't strangers to top-notch service, they all recognized that this gesture was Jemarious's attempt at making an impression on Tanya.

Winter thought it was cute and kept her eye on him all night, watching how he interacted with fans, with the other woman, and with Tanya. First observation was that he was very appreciative of his fans' support and didn't complain once about signing an autograph or snapping a flick. Her next observation, and an important one for her, was that he did not give any attention to the groupies and half-dressed women who were desperately vying for his attention. "Finally, she was loving how attentive and genuine he was with Tanya. He checked on her all night, making sure she was having a good time and that she didn't want for anything. He danced with her, grinded on her while also remaining a gentleman and not giving off the impression that he was not only after after her goods. They had a great time. The music was amazing, and they danced all night long.

The Party Ain't Over

Jemarious reserved a black SUV to take them back to their hotel. However, Taryn was hungry and asked if they could make a stop before the hotel. Of course, eager to continue to make a good impression on Tanya. And as a part of his southern hospitality, Jemarious hopped in and said, "Of course! Where would you like to go?"

Tanya was secretly happy that Taryn made her request as she wasn't quite ready to leave him, yet didn't want him to know it. They pulled up to Empanada Mama on Allen Street and hopped out to grab a batch of deliciously prepared empanadas and a few bottles of water, then hopped back in the truck to head to the hotel. They all ripped into their food and enjoyed the savory flavors of their fare. Jemarious had never eaten an empanada before and was pleasantly surprised at how delicious they were.

"Taryn, thank you for suggesting. These joints right here got a dude feeling like he got the munchies after puffing on that ooohh weee!" They all burst into laughter.

He is cute and funny. Hmmmm . . ., Tanya thought to herself with a secret smile.

They arrived at the hotel and climbed out of the SUV, intoxicated and full. Jemarious gave each of them a hug; his hug was especially longer with Tanya.

"Good night, ladies. It was a pleasure hanging with you all tonight. I had a ball! Be safe." He got back in the SUV, and as the driver pulled off, he rolled down the tinted window and stole one last look at Tanya. She stood curbside, staring back. Her gaze was interrupted when Winter blurted out, "Somebody got a crush!"

Tanya jokingly scoffed at her, "No, I don't. Girl, stop!" She rolled her eyes and laughed.

"Well, I wasn't talking about you . . . BUTTTT if the shoe fits . . ."

They all laughed.

Just then, Mia's cell rang. She smiled when she saw Toby's name on the caller ID. "Mia speaking," she answered, trying to hide her eagerness to pick up.

"Hey, Mia. Just checking to see if you all had fun tonight," he asked in a caring voice.

Warmly pleased at the display of care and concern for her, Mia responded, "Yes, we did. We actually just pulled up in front of the hotel." She bit her bottom lip and continued, "It would have been nice to have seen you tonight."

The girls whipped their heads around and stared down Mia's throat as she held her conversation. Tanya pinched Winter's arm and inquired, "Did this chick really just say that?"

Just as surprised, Winter responded, "I wouldn't believe it if I didn't hear it with my own ears."

Taryn yelled out, "Right, Mia . . . get that dick!"

Winter and Tanya cracked up laughing. Mia smiled and gritted her teeth. "Tarynnnn." She elongated her name. They all laughed again. Toby even snickered on the other end of the line. He enjoyed the interaction and exchanges between Mia and her friends. It was evident that they were as close as sisters and thoroughly enjoyed one another's company. There was a mutual love and respect, and they certainly busted one another's chops for shits and giggles. Toby missed this with his best buddies with whom he grew up in the small city of Annecy, France. They were now all domicile in cities across the globe.

"I can make that happen if you want me to," he responded.

Without hesitation, Mia responded a simple, Yes. Twenty minutes later, Toby pulled up in a sleek smoke-gray Aston Martin. He stepped out and gave each of them a hug before opening the passenger door for Mia. She kissed them each on the cheek and waved, bye.

Before she could say anything, Taryn exclaimed, "See you in the AM! Hopefully, you can walk!"

Mia rolled her eyes, and they all laughed. After Toby pulled off, Tanya said, "My turn! And Win . . . not tonight, chick. I don't wanna hear it!" Anticipating that once Winter found out that she was planning on meeting with Jackson, she'd be ready to get on her case.

Winter rolled her eyes. "Do what you want. You know he ain't worth shit, and I ain't gotta tell you that. But I cannot wait until you realize how good Jemarious will be for you so that you can leave Jackson's ass alone. Good night. I'm going to the room. I do not want to be here when his ass arrives," she scoffed and walked inside of the hotel. Taryn waited with Tanya for Jackson to arrive.

"T, you know she's right," she gently said to Tanya. Tanya just shrugged.

I know she's right. I don't know why I keep doing this to myself. She shook off the thought.

Jackson pulled up in an all-black Range Rover and waved to Taryn as he got out to open the door for Tanya. Taryn barely waved back.

"See you in the morning, Sis. Call me if you need anything . . . even if it's for me to come shoot a bitch," she said, staring directly at Jackson.

***

As Toby pulled into his underground parking garage, he turned down the Kenny G tunes ringing through the speakers, looked over at Mia, and smiled.

He found himself thinking, *She is such a beautiful woman. I'd do anything to make her happy.* He eased out of the car, walked around, opened the door, and gently held Mia's hand as she stepped out. With the touch of his hand, Mia felt a throb between her legs. They took the elevator up to the top floor. As they entered his penthouse, Toby dropped his jacket on the sofa and hurried off to the kitchen, yelling behind him, "Make yourself at home!"

Mia took off her Jimmy Choo heels and sat comfortably on the sofa. He walked back into the living room with a small cake in his hands and one lit candle. The cake read, *"Congratulations, Mia! Job well done!"* Mia felt a lump in her throat.

"Blow out the candle," he encouraged her. "You don't want it to melt onto your cake. It's vanilla cheesecake . . . your favorite."

Wow. He remembered that? Mia thought as she blew out the candle. Then she arose and planted a soft kiss on his lips. He pulled two forks from behind his back and handed her one. "Shall we?"

They began to dig into the cake. It was delicious; they cleaned the small plate. Toby leaned across Mia to sit the plate on the rustic end table. As he began to retract to his original position, she softly kissed him on his lips. He reciprocated and kissed her back softly and fervently. He stood her up and slowly slid her dress up and over her head, leaving her La Perla underwear exposed. He lifted her as she wrapped her legs around his waist and carried her into his bedroom. He laid her on his California king-sized bed, stepped back, and glossed over her body.

"Mia, you are so beautiful." He let the words escape his mouth. He leaned over her and began kissing her forehead down to her neck while she slid his T-shirt up and over his head. As he stood, she sat up with him, kissing his chest and helping him untie his lounge pants. His pants fell to his ankles, and to her pleasant surprise, he didn't have on any underwear. He stepped out from his pants and climbed onto the bed next to her. She turned onto her side to face him, and they locked eyes for a moment.

Toby could see the gloss of tears in Mia's eyes and wanted to do anything he could to take her sadness away. He leaned in and pecked the tip of her nose and smiled at her. Just then her heart cracked open, and she allowed herself to indulge in the emotion she felt running through her. Toby reached around her and unhooked her bra and began to softly kiss her breast. Mia hadn't felt such sensuality in a long time.

He then reached down and glided her panties down her legs. She helped him by lifting out one leg at a time. After slipping on his Magnum, he climbed on top of her and slowly entered her sweetness.

They both moaned in ecstasy. He gripped her hips and propelled himself deeper into her abyss. He slowly grinded and slid in and out, penetrating her deeper each time. Mia moaned with each movement. She wrapped her legs around his waist as she didn't want him to move too far away from her. She ran her fingers through his jet-black hair while he kissed her neck and nibbled on her ear. They enjoyed being intertwined and connected to each other. Then Toby felt his peak explosion coming on and began to pump faster and faster, making sure to hit Mia's G-spot. He squeezed her ass tight, pulling her onto his manhood with every stroke. Mia tossed her head back and let her long tresses fall onto the bed. Her legs began to tremble, and she squeezed her legs around him in a vice grip.

Toby thrust inside of her and exploded. They both fell on the bed, exhausted from their encounter, with sweat dripping from their bodies. Toby wrapped his arms around her as she laid her head on his chest. He didn't want to let her go.

***

Tanya and Jackson made their way to the Ritz-Carlton. She was unusually quiet.

"What's good, Ma?" Jackson asked.

"Nothing. I'm good," she responded, distracted from her thoughts. For the entire ride, she couldn't stop thinking about the night and partying with Jemarious.

Why am I here? I love me some Jackson, but he ain't no good for me. Jemarious seems like everything I would want and need in a man. They pulled up to the valet, Jackson hopped out, handed the keys to the attendant, ran around and opened the door for Tanya.

I mean, it's not like Jax doesn't treat me like a lady. But his damn addiction to the street life and women always gets in the way. And then when he brings that shit into my circles . . . now that's when things get messy. Tanya frowned a little at the thought of Jackson's inability to let go of his street lifestyle; not even if it meant he'd lose her.

They walked into the elevator, and as the doors closed behind them, Jackson leaned her up against the elevator wall, face first, and began grinding on her ass and kissing on her neck. She felt the moisture build between her legs and winded her ass in the same rhythm as his grind.

"Damn, Ma! I miss this ass so much," he whispered in her ear.

"I bet you do," she confidently responded.

They exited the elevator on the twenty-second floor and headed toward Jackson's suite. He walked directly behind her with his arms wrapped around her shoulders. As soon as they entered the room and locked the door, he leaned her up against the wall, kissed her and caressed her breast. She held both sides of his face in her hands and kissed him with the same intensity. He slid her skirt up and guided his hands between her velvet skin and silk underwear, and put his fingers inside of her. She let out a moan as he slid his fingers in deeper, thrusting them into her love. She twirled her hips and guided her love around them.

Jackson knew how to make Tanya cum just by using his hands. He slowed down the movement and allowed his thumb to tickle her clitoris.

She called out, "Yeah, Jax! Yess! Right there!"

Jackson's pride and joy was full and hard, and he grinded himself against her thigh while his fingers were working. He briskly pulled his hand out, unbuttoned and unzipped his jeans, pulling his penis out the top of his boxer briefs. He slid her panties to the side, and as he attempted to push himself inside of her, Tanya stopped him and requested, "Jax, please, put on a condom."

As much as Tanya loved him, she certainly didn't want any pregnancy accidents. He didn't resist and reached for the condom in his back pocket. He slid it on and thrust himself inside of her. He pumped hard and deep, grabbing her ass and separating her cheeks. Knowing that exposed more space for him to dig deeper.

Tanya thrust her hips forward to meet his manhood and squeezed her love around him. He tilted his head, bit down on her breast with his lips and let himself go. Once emptied, he lifted her around him and walked her to the sofa. He sat her on top of him, and she took control, propelling herself up and down on his manhood. He laid his head back and enjoyed the ride. He placed his fingers on her clitoris while she moved up and down. He knew how playing with her clitoris drove her crazy. Tanya felt her pleasure mounting and slowly grinded her hips in a circular motion, allowing her clitoris to be completely stimulated at the touch of his hands. She felt a warm sensation consume her body and allowed herself to wallow in it. Jackson didn't miss this opportunity to let himself loose again. Exhausted from their episode, he stretched himself across the sofa, and Tanya rested on top of him. They laid like this for the next hour until Tanya suggested they get up, shower, and get in the bed.

The Morning After

Mia opened her eyes to see the sun rising. She peeked over at the clock; it read 6:03 a.m. She smiled, feeling Toby's arms wrapped around her and allowed herself to melt into him.

"Good morning," he greeted her and kissed her on the forehead.

"Good morning," she softly replied. They smiled at each other as time stood still. The silence was broken when Mia's phone rang.

"Morning, chick. Are you going to make it to church this morning?" Taryn said with a sarcastic chuckle as if she knew what Mia was doing all night.

Mia chuckled. "Yes. Gonna head to the hotel now." She let out a sigh as she hung up the phone, feeling an overwhelming sense of sadness, knowing this personal time with Toby was ending. "I have to go now." She spoke softly.

"I know," he concurred.

Did I already mention this to him? "Yeah . . . the girls and I have plans to attend church this morning."

Toby leaned in and kissed her softly before they climbed out of bed. He walked in his closet and backed out with a big box in tow and handed the box over to her. "This is for you. I had Tanya help me with this."

Mia looked slightly confused but eager to open the package. Inside was a pale pink La Perla bra and panty set, a light gray suit from White House Black Market, a pale-pink silk blouse, a pair of patent leather Michael Kors pumps, and a toiletry bag with all the usual feminine products of her choice, a comb, a brush set, hair clips, and a bottle of Marc Jacobs Daisy perfume.

"Oh my gosh!" She let out a gasp, completely and pleasantly surprised at the well-organized and well-thought-out gesture.

When did he and Tanya plan all this? How did he know I'd even be here this morning? How did Tanya know? Her thoughts ran wild, trying to figure out when he and Tanya planned all of this and how it was pulled together so quickly. After all, they'd only met two days prior.

As if he were reading her mind, he spoke up, "I'll tell you one day how and when Tanya and I planned this. But I will say that your friend is quite amazing."

Mia nodded at his sentiment regarding Tanya. "Well, thank you! Both of you!" She smiled as she headed off to the shower.

Toby laid in bed and watched attentively as Mia got dressed. *She's so beautiful.* He admired her from his bed. As she pulled her hair into a bun, Toby got up; grabbed and pulled on some lounge pants, a T-shirt, and sneakers, and grabbed his car keys.

***

Toby reached over and held Mia's hand on the drive to the hotel. The ride was quiet as they were both engulfed in their own thoughts. They pulled up in front of the Mandarin. Toby leaned over and laid a soft and gentle kiss on Mia's lips, climbed out of the car, ran over, and opened her door. "I had a wonderful time, Mia."

She wrapped her arms around his neck. "As did I."

"I'll have your clothes cleaned and get them to you this week." With one last peck on the lips, Toby got in his car and drove away.

As Mia was walking into the hotel, she was interrupted by the sound of a beeping horn. She turned to look back and saw Tanya waving to her out the window of a black Range Rover. Mia waved back and waited for her friend. She was completely shocked when she saw Jackson walk around the truck to open Tanya's door.

"What's good, Mia? Congrats on making partner," Jackson hollered at her.

"Thanks" was all she could muster up at that moment. Her gaze was on Tanya the entire time, inquisitive about how and why she was with him.

They walked into the suite and found Taryn up, listening to Kirk Franklin bellow through the air and Winter on the phone with one of the vendors she used for her bed-and-breakfast.

"Well, good morning, ladies," Taryn said with a huge grin on her face. "Mia, you look refreshed and cute."

Mia thanked her. She then turned to Tanya and said, "And, thank *you* too!"

Tanya sarcastically smiled and said, "You're wellllcommee," curled her lips, and batted her eyes.

Mia laughed. "I'll tell y'all later how our girl pulled off the cutest scheme with Mr. Toby."

Prayer And Praise

They walked into church, took seats, and sang along with the choir until the pastor took his place at the altar. As the pastor preached, each of the ladies praised and prayed. They held one another's hands and prayed together.

Church was definitely a release for each of them. They were real with themselves, with one another, and with God. They wholeheartedly believed that He knew their weaknesses, their temptations, their mistakes, their fears, and their love for Him.

Mia sobbed as she asked God to forgive her transgression. She wanted out of her marriage, and God knew her struggle—how patient she'd been with Morris, how much she sacrificed her own happiness to try and prove to him that she could be all he wanted her to be as a mother and wife while still pursuing her career goals, and how she ignored the fact that she knew he had been having an affair for the last two years. She thanked God for having her wonderful children, for making partner, and for blessing her with such supportive and genuine friends.

Taryn wept and prayed for guidance, courage, and discernment. She asked God to guide her and show her if she's made the right decision to move to Vegas with Chase. She prayed that Alana and Ryan would be OK with the decision and that the move wouldn't be hard on them. She asked God to help her learn to fully trust again and give Chase a fair chance because she believed he truly loved her. She thanked God for her friends, their support. and their love.

Tanya held back her tears as she prayed for her mother. She asked God to heal her if it were possible but, if not, to please give them more time together. She asked for the strength to go and see her without completely breaking down and prayed for courage to get through this. She thanked God for her friends. She asked for forgiveness and for backtracking with Jackson and to help her find the strength to leave him alone. God knew he wasn't good for her.

Winter's tears flowed as she prayed for her children and their life without their father. She asked God to get a message to Tim in Heaven, letting him know that she and the kids missed him but were doing fine. She thanked God for her friends and for all their support. She prayed that God would continue to bless her business and her prosperity and asked for guidance on that path she should be taking while setting up her second establishment. She even thanked God for sending Charlie into her life. She asked that he help her to keep her mind and heart open if there was an opportunity for true love.

They felt peace.

Home Sweet Home

After church, they headed to Mia's for lunch before everyone departed. Mia had lunch catered by one of their favorite soul-food restaurants. The kids were happy to see them and eager to tell them all about the fun they had over the weekend—from the Friday evening trip out to iPlay America in New Jersey, to the day spent at CoCo Key, surprise seafood dinner with Uncle Morris, the late nights up, the games, and all the goodies Louisa and Morris let them indulge throughout the weekend.

Winter and Taryn's black SUV arrived shortly after lunch. They said their goodbyes and rallied the kids for the airport. Before leaving, Winter reminded Mia to book her trip down to South Carolina so that they could start interviewing and taste-testing with the individuals who applied for the master chef position at the new bed-and-breakfast.

Tanya chimed in, "Mia, let's plan our dates at the same time so that I can look at the space and develop some design ideas."

Winter agreed, "That'll work."

Tanya's flight was later that evening as she planned to spend a few hours visiting her mom at the hospice.

"Give Ma a kiss for me," Taryn instructed on her way out the door.

"Me too!" Winter added.

***

The house was quiet as Taryn and Alana entered. *Ryan must still be at Kayla's house.* She sat their luggage in the laundry room. *I'll unpack and wash later.*

Alana ran up to her room, screaming, "My bed! My bed!"

Taryn chuckled. *That is my child! She loves sleep as much as I do.* She was still joyful from the weekend trip and seeing her besties. *It was so nice seeing my girls. I love that my chicks are doing their thing,* she thought to herself and smiled, while also wishing they lived closer.

Shucks! I'm about to live even further from them. She instantly recalled her recent decision to move to Las Vegas with Chase. Right on cue, her cell phone rang. She smiled as Chase's name flashed on her screen.

"Hey, babe," she answered with glee.

"Hey, you! Making sure you and Alana made it home safely," Chase inquired.

"Yes. We made it here safely." Her tone became slightly somber.

"What's up? What's the matter, babe?" he asked, concerned. Before she could answer, he continued, "You know what, babe? Tell me about it when I get there. I'll be there in about thirty minutes."

Taryn immediately perked up. Her heart fluttered from the excitement of seeing Chase. "OK, babe. Let me get Alana and I settled in. I'll order some Chinese food. Oh, and can you call Ryan? Maybe you can pick her up on your way here."

Chase smiled. He could hear the excitement in her voice. He loved making her happy, and it made him happy just knowing she was so excited to see him. "OK! Love you. See you shortly."

Taryn danced through the house, getting her and Alana prepared for the coming work and school week. *Damn! I love that man. I love me some Chase Durr! I can't wait to see him.*

***

Winter and the kids made a pit stop at her office before heading home. She needed to grab a few resumes which she wanted to look over for the hotel manager and guest-services manager positions she had posted for her new location.

Tiffany and TJ loved going to the bed-and-breakfast. The staff treated them like royalty, and they loved the delicious cheesecake that was always available for their taking.

"Come on guys! We have to get going. The car is still outside waiting on us," she called out to the twins from the back of the kitchen."

They hurried to their mom's side after downing their last pieces of cheesecake. They arrived home and headed straight for the shower. Winter unloaded their bags and dropped everything in the wash, except for the items needing to go to the cleaners. She organized that stuff into the basket she maintained for professional cleaning. She then headed upstairs to hop in the shower.

She found herself thinking, *I want to call Charlie,* but pushed the thought to the back of her mind. After having dinner with the twins and getting them off to bed, she poured a glass of wine, sat on the sofa, put on some smooth jazz, and began reading through and marking up the resumes. Once done, she sat the papers down and allowed herself to indulge in her thoughts of Charlie.

He is so fine and sexy. I feel bad about what his ex-girl did, but welp! She left him available for me. I hope Tim isn't upset with me in heaven. I know he'd want me to be happy. I wonder if Charlie is spending this much time thinking about me. She immersed herself in her thoughts until she dozed off to sleep.

Give Notice

It was the last day of school. The air was buzzing with the excitement of the kids anticipating no more homework, classwork, and teachers for an entire two months. The teachers—well, some—were just as excited and looking forward to the break. Taryn was buzzing from her own excitement and anticipation of meeting with her colleagues and staff to inform them of her decision to relocate to Las Vegas. After all the students were dismissed into their summer freedom, she entered the auditorium where her boss, colleagues, and staff were congregating.

Mr. Sheldon, her boss, summoned her to the front of the room. He cleared his throat to get their attention.

"Good afternoon, all. Let's get started so that we don't hold anyone back from starting their summer break. It is with mixed emotions that I announce that our friend and colleague, Ms. Taryn Jackson, has informed me of her decision to resign as she and her daughters will be moving to Nevada this summer, where she also plans to pursue her lifelong dream of opening her own charter school."

There were gasps of surprise in the room and inquisitive stares. Taryn stood next to Mr. Sheldon, straight-faced, not in the mood to answer a whole bunch of questions.

Who told him to tell my business? I didn't ask him to tell anyone about my charter school. Taryn didn't mind sharing the information about her plans, but she certainly wanted to be the one who shared it.

***

The last month and a half had been full of planning, packing, and getting her house sufficiently listed on the market. Alana and Ryan spent every second they could with their friends and made promises to visit as often as they could, knowing they'd be able to since their grandparents would remain residents in the area. Chase spent nearly the entire last month with them, making sure to assist with packing since Taryn refused his offer to have a moving company help. She was very particular about her belongings and wanted to handle everything. She donated all her and the girls' furniture and a few boxes of clothing, had the painters come and paint the walls white so that potential buyers would see a clean palette and had her realtor set up staging for an open house. Chase had her trade in her Mercedes Benz truck and had the dealer make arrangements for a new truck for her to pick up in Vegas.

"Today is the day, girls!" Taryn announced the obvious to her daughters. Alana and Ryan were excited. It pleased both Taryn and Chase to see that that they were handling the move so well.

"I can't wait to see my room!" Ryan exclaimed. She looked at Alana and teased, "Mr. Chase said I have my *own* bathroom, walk-in closet, and he had a floor-to-ceiling mirror set up in it!"

Alana rolled her eyes and responded, "So what? I have my *own* bathroom too! *And* I have a queen-sized bed plus a sofa in my room. That means my room is *big*!" They both started laughing.

Taryn looked at Chase and smiled. "You're going to have these girls so spoiled."

He shrugged. "Well, why not? I have their mother spoiled. Besides, I just want the best for my girls." He leaned in and kissed her on the cheek. "Our ride is outside. Let's go, girls," Chase called out.

As they headed out the door, Taryn turned, took one last look over her house, and locked the door for the last time.

Love Blossoms

Winter and Charlie's romance blossomed since she returned from her weekend trip in New York City. She realized that she couldn't spend the rest of her life holding on to Tim. She knew he wouldn't want her to be lonely and missing out on life. Charlie was a gentleman and treated her like a queen. He had a gentle southern charm and yet the presence of a chiseled giant. Winter felt safe and comfortable when they were together. She found herself sharing her fears and her dreams with him. He was attentive, thoughtful, and caring. She called him her "gentle giant." He laughed every time she referred to him as such, knowing that his fellow officers would bust his balls over it.

***

The day she received the call from her realtor that the sellers of the property she wanted had accepted her offer and conditions, she was having lunch with Charlie. She jumped out of her seat with joy and found herself wrapping her arms around his neck. She was elated that he was there when she received the news. After all, he had endured her nervous rants for the past few weeks.

"OMG! They accepted my offer! I just knew they were going to say *no*, thinking it was too low based off what they were asking and especially since the last place I had lined up fell through. OMG! Thank you, God! Thank you!" she exclaimed. Charlie held her back and smiled. He was extremely happy for her and loved seeing her so thrilled.

She pulled back and genuinely asked Charlie, "I need to get over to the realtor's office now. She wants me to sign some papers. Can you go with me?"

"Of course! My next shift isn't until 11:00 p.m. I'm free to go wherever you need me to," he warmly responded. As Charlie escorted her to her realtor's office, she reached over in his truck and held his hand.

"Thank you! Thank you for being here . . . with me . . . in my life . . . at this very moment." She smiled and remained quiet the remainder of the drive.

Winter spent the next hour signing all the paperwork, while Charlie waited in the truck. She exited the building and headed toward his truck, with a huge smile on her face. He got out to open the door for her but instead found himself in her warm embrace as she ran to him and landed right in his arms.

"I am so happy right now. We close tomorrow. This is really happening! I can't wait to tell the girls. Mia and Tanya are planning to come down in a few weeks. They'll get to see the space. I hope they love it as much as I do. I can't wait until you see it too. You're going to love it. I hope you're ready 'cause we will be spending a lot of time there over the next couple of years." She stopped, realizing that she was not only rambling, but also planning to have a future with Charlie. She looked up at him, not only looking for amicability on his face but also fearing that she'd just scared him away.

To her pleasure, he was smiling and nodding. Then he added, "I'm sure we will have fun doing all that we need to do to get the bed-and-breakfast to the level of success as the other, which, for you, babe, won't be too hard."

Babe, she noted.

He helped Winter into the truck and asked, "Where to, Ms. Jones?"

She laughed at him imitating a chauffeur. "To my office, Mr. Howard."

He submitted.

***

Charlie walked Winter up to her office. "I'm very happy for you, Ms. Winter Jones. You are a phenomenal woman."

Winter could no longer hold back her desire. She grabbed him by the hand and guided him toward her personal room. As they entered, Charlie leaned in and began kissing her on the neck from behind. She pressed her ass into his groin and subtly grinded on him. She could feel his nature rise and focused on the pressure up against her ass. Charlie slid his hands up her blouse and began caressing her breast. He kissed her deeper as he felt her areola stiffen at his touch. He began to grind back on her ass as she pressed in closer and pressed his back up against the wall.

In one swift 180-degree turn, him now had her chest pressed up against the wall, and his hands were slowly sliding up her knee-length pencil skirt. Winter swayed her hips left and right, helping aid the skirt past her curvaceous hips. He unbuttoned his pants and let them drop to his ankles. He then eased down his boxer briefs, slid her panties to the side, and pushed himself into her. He wrapped his hands on her thighs to steady himself as he pumped in and out of her. She pushed herself onto his love with each pump. Her hands were pressed up against the wall, helping her to powerfully thrust herself onto him. He then quickly turned her around, lifted her up around his waist, and pressed her back up against the wall. She swathed her legs around his waist and arched her back, and he continued to move himself inside of her.

Winter's hands were pressed on his shoulders as she dug her nails into his skin. His hands cupped her ass and assisted her up and down on his manhood. She squeezed her warmth around him as she felt herself cum. He could no longer hold back and erupted. As he lowered her to the floor, she held her arms around his neck. He enveloped his arms around her waist. They maintained their embrace for a few minutes before he helped replace her clothing on her body and then organized his own.

Winter's eyes welled up with tears. Charlie immediately noticed and put his arms around her. "What's the matter? Why are you crying?" he asked with sincere concern in his voice.

She spoke softly. "I haven't made love to anyone since Tim died. I haven't had feelings for anyone since he died. I vowed that I'd never let myself fall for anyone ever again. Losing is just too painful. And besides, who would treat me as special as Tim? And then here you come, strolling into my office, helping a patron find their pet, catching me as I almost bust my behind when I stumbled down the steps." She chuckled and continued, "I have found myself trying to find something wrong with you, tried to convince myself that you were too good to be true. But the more I tried to see something wrong, the more you continued to show me your heart of gold. You continue to make me feel special and beautiful. Even after you've been hurt, you have allowed me space in your heart."

"I want you, Mr. Charles Howard. I want you in my life. If this is too much for you, please let me know. If me having two children is too much for you to invest in, please let me know. I promise I won't be mad. But I certainly would be upset with myself if I didn't at least tell you how I felt. I don't believe it takes a long time to love someone. I won't waste anymore of my life holding on to pain and allow myself to hold back on my true feelings."

Her tears began to stream. Charlie wiped her eyes. "Winter, I'm not going anywhere. I'm right here and am completely invested in you and all that comes along with that. You are a breath of fresh air. My career puts me in very dangerous situations, and I know that scares you. I promise to be cautious, and I hope you are willing to be with me. I'm here, Winter. I'm not going anywhere."

Houston Is Home

It's been a few weeks since Tanya's been back in Houston. She was still surrounded by a few unpacked boxes, but her new place was coming along nicely. Ethan Allen delivered her sofa and lounge chair timely. The custom-designed window dressings were installed. Her Mediterranean-style California King bedposts and mattresses were set up, and her walk-in closet was already organized with her full wardrobe. She loved the size of her closet. It gave her more of a reason to continue buying things to put in it. It was beginning to feel like home.

She plopped on her sofa with a bottle of SmartWater and scrolled through her Instagram time line. She spotted a picture of Jemarious in a pair of basketball shorts and no shirt, palming a ball with one hand. The caption read, "Ball all day!" She noticed a few comments from his friends, agreeing with him, and several comments from chicks on his body, his looks, and how much they'd like to be with him or what they'd do to him.

Ugh. I can't stand groupie bitches. She dropped her phone on the sofa got up and searched out her workout clothes. *Let me get to the gym. Today is the only day I don't have any meetings or other plans. I'm going to work out, grab me some fruit, water, and salmon, and get my behind back in this house to relax. Yup, that's going to be my day,* Tanya thought as she pulled on a pair of Adidas leggings, a sports bra, and her favorite running sneakers. She pulled her hair into a ponytail and threw on a cap.

She grabbed her phone off the sofa and noticed she had a missed call from Jemarious. She hit the redial key without thinking. He picked up on the first ring.

"Hey, Ms. Mack. What's good? What you up to?"

Tanya smirked and answered, "I'm good. About to head to the gym. What's good with you?"

"Oh OK. I see. You gotta keep that body tight! I'm not mad at that. I'm chillin' today and wanted to see if you wanted to grab something to eat," he responded.

She hesitated a little before she answered. He was strategic in ensuring that he drew clear lines between their professional relationship and the personal relationship he was seeking to have. He always went through her assistant when it came to business matters and he only called her directly whenever it was nonbusiness related. This became his strategic approach over the last few weeks—the few times when they'd met for lunch, movies, dinner, and drinks.

Tanya enjoyed Jemarious's company. He was cool, funny, humble, and wasn't constantly trying to push up on her. He made it known that he liked her and would like things to develop into something more between them but completely respected her stand on not dating her clients and understood this meant he had to move slow and convincingly if he were to get her to change her perspective.

"Sure. But instead of going out, you feel like grabbing something and chilling at my house?" *Oh shit! Did I just invite him to my house?* "I could use some help unpacking the rest of these damn boxes," she added, trying not to sound like she was excited about him coming over.

He laughed. "OK. Cool. Hit me up on your way back from the gym. I'll grab some Thai food and come over."

***

The gym was quite empty. This was her first time working out at the site since she signed up the week she moved into the area.

It's kind of empty in here. I thought there'd be more people, especially since it was packed the day I signed up. But good. I'm not in the mood for a lot of people anyway. Tanya worked up a good sweat for forty-five minutes before heading to the local market to pick up the fruit, water, and salmon she had on her shopping list. She hopped in her I8 and hit the Bluetooth to call Jemarious. She was annoyed when he didn't answer the phone.

Oh no. See, I don't play this game. Don't tell me call you when I'm done and then you don't answer. She didn't bother to leave a message. She thought about sending a text but convinced herself not to.

Yeah . . . no . . . I'm not one of these thirsty ass chicks who's gonna hunt him down. Nah . . . I'm good, she thought to herself. As she pulled up to her house, she noticed a red, white, and black Harley-Davidson Fat Boy in her driveway. She instantly smiled when she recognized Jemarious as he took off his helmet, dug in a compartment on his bike and, pulled out two bags of food. She gestured for him to follow her into the garage as she pulled her car in. *OK. That's why he couldn't answer.*

Jemarious was impressed at Tanya's house. "This is a nice place, Ms. Mack! I likes," he complimented as he walked in through the garage door.

"The kitchen is to your left." She pointed. "I'm going to hop in the shower real quick. Get comfortable."

Tanya headed straight to the bathroom to freshen up. Jemarious took the liberty to organize the remaining boxes in her livingroom by their respective labeling and slid them up against the wall. He also placed her flat-screen TV on the wall mounts that had already been installed and hooked up all the wiring to the cable box and modem. He found the small box labeled 'CORDS AND STUFF' and he chuckled at the label but figured that's where he'd most likely find the remote; he was right.

Tanya entered the living room, garbed in a pair of leggings, a white fitted tank top, and some fuzzy slippers. Her hair was pulled up in a bun, and her face glowed from her face cream. She found Jemarious sitting on the sofa, watching television. She was pleasantly surprised to see how busy he'd kept himself while she showered.

"Thank you! You saved me from having to hire someone to come and put my TV up. It hadn't been delivered at the time the people came to put the wall mounts up." She noticed that it was a little warmer than usual in the house. "I need to crank up the central air. It's hot in here."

Jemarious informed her that he had turned the oven on and sat the food in it so that it didn't get cold. "Thai food tastes horrible when reheated in the microwave."

After they finished eating, Jemarious grabbed the plates, water bottles, and food containers and took everything into the kitchen. Tanya heard the dishwasher start and the garbage disposal chomp away.

Wow. He's handy, and he cleans up after himself. She leaned back on the sofa and stretched her legs onto the black-and-gold leather cocktail table. Jemarious walked back in and joked, "You got that itis!"

Tanya burst into laughter. He grabbed the remote and navigated to *on demand.*

"Whatchu wan' watch?" he asked with a southern drawl. They both agreed they wanted to watch something funny and decided on *Kevin Hart: What Now?*

***

They were tickled at the comedic rants spewing through the built-in surround sound speakers. Tanya took notice that Jemarious's phone hadn't rung much since he was there. She also took note at how he gave her his undivided attention whenever she spoke. He shared a few things about himself over their meal but was very humble and certainly didn't brag about himself or his money. Tanya tried hard not to allow herself to notice all these great qualities in him.

Mia and Winter would be screaming, I told you so, if they were here to witness this. Tanya pressed pause on the remote and turned to face him.

"So you know I'm single. I date and have my little excursions from time to time. I haven't been in a relationship in nearly five years. I have lost all my faith in men since Jackson, my ex I told you about at lunch. So why are you here?" she bluntly asked, surprising herself at how direct she was, but didn't regret it because she really wanted to know where he was coming from.

Jemarious was a bit surprised by the timing of her questions, but after hearing about her history with Jackson, he wasn't surprised that she held steady in the relationship status she was in and her lack of continuity with any of the men she occasionally went out with.

"Tanya. I don't have any expectations of you. I like spending time with you. You are down-to-earth, a hell of a businesswoman, beautiful, and smart. When I'm around you, I never feel like I have to second-guess if you're all about the fame and money, like most—no—*all* of these broads I encounter every day. I do like you. I would love to continue getting to know you. I don't want to stop spending time with you. And...would I like to get in those draws? OF COURSE! You are fine as hell! I mean . . . I am a man!"

Tanya giggled and appreciated his honesty. *Damn, T. Don't do it! Don't let yourself get caught up,* she scolded herself, already knowing that she was falling for him.

"Well, OK then" were the only words she could find. She reached for the remote, and he grabbed her wrist, pulling her closer to him. He leaned back on the sofa, allowing her to place her head on his chest as they continued to watch the remainder of the comedy show until they dozed off.

Calling It Quits

The last few weeks were quite a struggle for Mia and Morris. They'd agreed to separate after she confronted him about not caring to celebrate or even acknowledge her making partner. He told her outright that he could *not* celebrate something he was against in the first place. His words pierced her heart, and that's when she asked him to leave. She wasn't surprised when he immediately obliged, but she was worried about the impact it would have on their children.

They agreed to share the news with Mylie and Myles together to ensure that they understood that, despite the separation, they were loved by both Mom and Dad. Mia was surprised at how well their children handled the news. Morris was upset and surprised that they weren't more upset. He wanted them to be as angry as he was about their mom working instead of being home with them.

Mia hadn't told anyone but Toby and her aunt Joan about Morris's departure. She mentioned it to Toby one Sunday afternoon over lunch while the kids were visiting with their dad at his rented loft in the meatpacking district. Toby listened as she replayed the argument for him.

How can he be so damn dense? This woman is beautiful, smart, a great mother, and successful. What is this man's problem? But I'm glad he has a problem with it because that gives me an opportunity to be all that she needs, he'd thought to himself during the pauses of her story. Mia appreciated him just listening; that was all she needed at that moment.

***

Mia had shed her tears when she visited her aunt Joan and informed her she and Morris's decision to separate. She'd laid in bed beside her aunt while she rubbed her head.

"I can't believe he can be so selfish. I mean, even if he's not happy about me having a career, as a human being, he couldn't just say congratulations. I'm so mad at myself for staying in this marriage for so long and for staying, knowing his ass been having an affair for so long. I should have listened to you, Mommy, and Daddy when y'all tried to warn me. But then again, I wouldn't have my babies. They are the best things that came out of this marriage," Mia sobbed as she vented.

"Morris's ass is selfish. He is weak. He can't handle a strong woman like you. He needs someone to be completely dependent on him. Myles and Mylie will be OK, Mia. They are strong like their momma. And, Mia, my love, you and Morris have not been in a loving relationship for the past two years. Don't feel guilty about finding love somewhere else. Toby loves you, and anyone paying attention can see that. Allow yourself to love him back. You deserve it. Besides, I want to see and know you and Tanya are happy before I leave this earth."

Mia laid in her aunt's arm for a couple of hours. Her aunt Joan filled the void of Mia's mother since her parents retired to their dream ranch in Phoenix, Arizona. Although Mia spoke to her parent's multiple times each day, she missed being able to snuggle up underneath each of them when she felt sad, scared, or hurt.

A Year Of Blessings

This has been a rewarding year so far. My girl Mia, my bish, made partner. Win opened her second bed-and-breakfast. T Mack relocated to her dream city, and her clientele has doubled since being there. I'm out in here in Vegas—me and my babies—happy and with a man who treats me like royalty. Ryan has been accepted to UCLA on a full academic scholarship, and to top it off, my charter school is being built and should be ready for grand opening in September, and I met my student enrollment capacity, Taryn reflected on the year to date. She thanked God before rolling over to wrap her arms around Chase. She took in the peace and quiet of her new home. The house was so big that she often felt like she was in her own little sanctuary when in her bedroom.

Chase had the entire room made over with all the special touches she'd requested. He wanted to make sure she felt that this was her house as well. He even had the room extended so that she had her own walk-in closet. She kissed him on his forehead, climbed out of bed, and made her way downstairs to the kitchen.

Ryan and Alana were fast asleep in their rooms. They were not early risers like their mom, whose body arose at four thirty each morning like clockwork, for the last ten years. A few minutes later, she heard Chase walking into the kitchen behind her. As she was filling up her teapot with water, he eased up behind her and gently kissed her on the neck.

"I knew I'd find you down here." He lifted her night shirt and began rubbing her ass. He slid his finger in between her legs, from behind, and softly rubbed her sweetness. She spread her legs for easier access as he guided his rock-hard fullness into her. He leaned her onto the kitchen island and began pumping inside of her. Taryn backed her ass into him and quickly took the lead. He held on to her waist as she twirled and twerked her ass on him. He gritted his teeth in order to hold back the sounds of his pleasure.

Taryn whispered, "Yeah, Daddy."

Chase leaned in closer and rubbed her clitoris while she winded her ass on his manhood. She felt herself escalating to her climax. She immediately turned herself around and kneeled in front of him, taking all of him into her mouth. He trembled at the warm moisture around his hardness. He pulled back and exploded onto her breast. She stood and faced him head on.

He kissed her on her lips, smacked her ass, and said, “Bring me a cup of tea upstairs,” and laughed.

“OK. And have the thang standing up waiting on me,” she teased.

A Change Of Heart

Tanya spent an hour getting dressed for her dinner date with Jemarious. She conceded to a pair of skinny jeans with a classic Pigalle pump and a tank that met the top of her jeans perfectly. As she headed out the door, she complimented herself, *I'm rocking this comfy but cute outfit. Jemarious will be happy.*

She grabbed her nude Celine tote and walked to the black Bentley coupé parked outside of her house. Jemarious smiled as he watched her strut to his car before getting out to open the door for her.

"You look very nice, Ms. Mack."

Tanya thanked him and eased into the car. She loved the cream-colored leather seats and the cherrywood paneling. She worried that her jeans might stain the leather and asked Jemarious if she should sit on something. He assured her that the leather was treated and stain proof.

Jemarious was also casually and comfortably dressed in a pair of jeans, some black Gucci loafers, a simple white button-up with the sleeves rolled a third up his arm. He sported a fully iced Clé de Cartier skeleton watch.

He is so simple and always very casual. I love that he took my advice and followed through on the style. Although he was an extremely wealthy athlete, he was very humble, which was one of the characteristics she loved about him.

They enjoyed their delicious dinner at Monarch Bistro in Houston's Museum District. Jemarious took the liberty of ordering her drink.

He remembered how much I love a great apple martini, she thought to herself. They laughed and flirted throughout dinner, shared a few personal stories, and enjoyed each other's company. Tanya couldn't recall the last time she had this much fun on a date.

The evening was warm and had a romantic hue in the air. As they were leaving, Tanya asked Jemarious if he'd like to take a walk around the area; the Museum District and evening lights were soft and beautiful. He agreed, and they strolled several blocks, talking and laughing. He held her hand as they walked.

"Damn, my feet hurt! These pumps were made for looking cute, surely not for walking." They both laughed.

Jemarious bent and removed her shoes one foot at a time and handed them to her. Before should could open her mouth and state that she was not going to walk barefoot, he turned his back to her, kneeled, and told her, "Hop on."

Tanya mounted his back. He wrapped his arms around her legs to hold her steady and headed back toward the restaurant valet.

As they drove back to Tanya's place, he seemed to be lost in his thoughts. She noticed how quiet he was, and was curious to ask him what he was thinking about, but opted not to. Instead, she requested that he put some music on. He hit the audio button and pointed at the screen with his music library displayed. Tanya searched until she found a few old school tracks. LL Cool J's "I Need Love," Ready for the World's "Tonight," and, finally, Lisa and Cult Jam's, "Someone to Love Me for Me" glared through the speakers.

Jemarious pulled into the driveway in front of Tanya's house and turned to her. "Thank you for a fun night, Ms. Mack," before getting out of the car to open her door.

Damn, he didn't even wait for me to respond. He's rushing me now. Maybe he gotta go meet his next chick. This is exactly why I do me. I don't have time for this type of bullshit.

Jemarious reached for her hand to help her out of the car. She had an attitude, turned to grab her bag and shoes, and briskly brushed past him to go in her house. He reached and grabbed her by the wrist.

"What's the matter? Are you OK, Tanya?" he asked.

"I'm good. Had fun. Seems like you're in a rush, so don't let me hold you up," she snapped back.

He pulled her closer to him and took her other wrist into his hand. "Tanya, I don't have anywhere else I wanna be but right here with you."

Just then, she slid her hand down to grip his and led him into her house and straight to her bedroom.

***

Tanya dropped her shoes and bag at the entrance of her bedroom door and laid on her bed, pulling Jemarious down next to her. He began to kiss her slowly, caressing her neck then her breast, and worked his hand down to the top of her jeans. She assisted him in unbuttoning her jeans and lifting herself so that he could easily slide them past her hips, thighs, and then down her legs. He began slowly fingering her, bringing his finger up to his mouth to taste her passion and then go back for more. He eased himself down, pulled her thong off, and gently placed his tongue on her love. He switched back and forth between penetrating her with his fingers and suckling her clitoris.

Tanya was in ecstasy and twirled her hips to meet his tongue and fingers. She gripped the pillows on her bed as she reached her climax. He then removed his clothing, exposing his muscular physique and his chocolate thunder, fully girthed.

After strapping on his Magnum, he towered himself over her, pulled her tank top over her head, and unsecured her bra. Her breasts were full, round, and inviting. He began teasing her nipples with the tip of his tongue. This little gesture incited a burst of moisture between Tanya's legs, and she spread them wide inviting him to enter. He drove himself into her over and over. As she was about to climax, again, she thought to herself, *Damn, I'm going out like a punk.*

She quickly lifted her hips and flipped him over. She kissed him on the lips, brought herself up on the tips of her toes, and began to ride him. She slowly glided up and down at first, ensuring that she pulled up, all the way to his tip of his girth, and slid slowly back down so he was fully immersed in her. She could tell that this drove him crazy. He gripped her hips and began lifting her up and down faster and faster. He yelled out, "Damn, Tanya! Shiiiiiiiittttttt. I'm cumming . . . I'm cumming!"

He exploded. She dismounted him and plopped on the bed. They laid there, sweating and panting. He reached over, pulled her head onto his chest, wrapped his arm around her, and closed his eyes. Tanya rested there with her eyes opened for a few, thinking to herself and happy that she decided to listen to her girls and give him a chance.

The Call

Tanya's sleep was abruptly interrupted by the constant buzzing of her cell phone. She grabbed for it in the dark, knocking it to the floor.

"Shit!" She got up and noticed that she had five missed calls from Mia, two missed calls from Mia's mom, and a missed call from the hospice. Her heart sank. She immediately knew what the calls were about.

Please, God. NO! Please, God! She hesitated a minute and decided to call Mia back first. If this were bad news, Mia was the only person she would be able to take it from. Mia answered the phone, sounding like she had been weeping.

"T, have you spoken to anyone at the hospice? They called me after trying to reach you earlier."

Tanya quietly responded, "No. I called you back first. Mia, please . . . please don't tell me . . ." Tears began strolling down her face.

"T . . . T, I'm so sorry. Your mom . . . Auntie . . . she passed away about an hour ago. Looks like her heart gave out. They tried to resuscitate her, but it didn't work. T, I'm so sorry." Mia managed to get the words out in between sobs.

"Noooo, Mia! Nooooo! Mommyyyy!" Tanya uncontrollably squealed as tears streamed down her face. Jemarious was startled and jumped up out of his sleep.

"Tanya, what's the matter? What happened?" he asked. He saw the tears streaming down her face when he turned the lamp on and instantly knew the news she'd just received. He wrapped his arms around her, and she leaned into his chest, holding the phone to her ear.

"Mia, I don't know what to do, what to think. My heart, Mia . . . my heart. Noooo . . . Mommy." She wept. The pain in her heart felt as if someone had just stuck a dagger in it.

"I'm going to catch the next flight out. I'll meet you at the hospice."

Mia agreed. Once she hung up the phone, Jemarious generously offered, "I'll charter a plane for us, Tanya. Let me make a call."

Tanya quickly showered and dressed. She cried the entire time. Her heart was heavy, and she already began feeling lost without her mom. Jemarious informed her that they'd be able to fly out in an hour and a half. He hopped in the shower, threw on his clothes, and they headed to

Priority One Jets tarmac. As they boarded the plane, she held his hand, thankful that he was with her. The pilot informed them that they'd be touching down in New York in three hours and thirty-eight minutes.

***

Winter was up reading through some papers when her phone rang.

"Hey, Mia. What's up, girl? Everything OK?" She immediately realized that Mia was crying.

"Win, Aunt Joan passed away." She let out the words.

"Oh no! Mia, no! Where is Tanya?" she inquired as she began to sob.

"Jemarious chartered a flight for them. They're headed here now. Win, can you call her cousins and inform them? I just can't deal with a million dumbass questions right now, especially from Aunt Joan's brother who only cares about money."

Winter knew all too well how money hungry Tanya's uncle Mo and his kids were. They knew Mia would know the details of Aunt Joan's financial affairs as she had power of attorney and ensured her aunt's money was well invested and insurance policies were in place. While Tanya was extremely bright and financially savvy, her mom knew that she wouldn't be able to focus well when this time came. Therefore, they both agreed to have Mia assist with the management of her affairs.

"Sure, Mia. I'll let them know, hon. I love you, Sis. Let me call Tanya and then these folks. Will call you back shortly."

Next, Mia called Taryn. Chase answered her phone. "Hey, Mia. It's Chase. Taryn is in the shower and asked me to pick up."

He heard the sorrow in Mia's voice and rushed into the bathroom, alarming Taryn. "T, I think you need to take this call," he urged.

Taryn stepped out of the shower and grabbed the phone. "Mia, what's wrong?"

Before Mia could get her words out, she began crying hard. Taryn instantly began to cry without know exactly why Mia was crying.

"Mia, what happened? Something with Morris? The kids? What happened?" she nervously asked through her tears. Chase stood in the bathroom; his eyes were locked on Taryn.

"Auntie Joan . . ." was all Mia could get out. She and Taryn cried in each other's ear. Taryn sat on the toilet and held her head with one hand and the phone to her ear in the other.

"Mia . . . Tanya . . . she's not going to be able to handle this. Oh my God. Aunt Joan. Oh God!" They cried together for the next twenty minutes.

"I'm going up to the hospice. Tanya should be there in a few hours. I need to start whatever paperwork they need. T, this is so hard. Damn! I have to call my parents. My mom is losing it . . . her best friend is gone . . .," Mia cried even harder, heartbroken from the loss and having to be there for her own mother.

"Mia, I'm so sorry, Mama. I love you so much. Please let me know if there's anything I can do. I'm going to call Tanya now. I can only imagine how she's taking this. I'll call you back later."

Taryn hung up and flew into Chase's arms. She pressed her head into his chest and cried. He stood there, holding her.

It's Hard To Say Goodbye

Joan Mack was well-known and respected in the entertainment and fashion industries. She was the stylist to some of the most well-known celebrities of her time. It was no wonder that her funeral was such a high-profile event. She loved things that were big and grand, as that's how she lived her life. She wanted to be cremated and have pictures of herself with her clients, family, and friends framed in gold and diamond frames, spread throughout the funeral home. She wanted people not only to remember and admire her fashion sense, but to also pay homage to those who were a part of her life.

There were so many fond memories brought to life in the pictures displayed. There wasn't a dry eye in the room, but there were also tons of smiles through the tears as people shared stories about the wonderful life of Joan Mack. Pictures of her and Tanya were plentiful. They were two peas in a pod, and Tanya was certainly a splitting image of her mom.

Jemarious sat by Tanya's side the entire duration of the viewing as she squatted in the first seat directly in front of the huge urn holding her mother's ashes. She politely smiled and hugged everyone as they greeted her and shared their condolences. She kept her sunglasses over her eyes as her tears and sleepless nights had brought them to a puffy swell.

Taryn and Winter sat in the seats directly behind Tanya as they endured the sadness they felt, both for losing Aunt Joan and the heaviness they knew Tanya felt. Chase and Charlie sat on either side of them, holding their hands for comfort. Mia sat with her parents in the adjacent front row. She and her mom were on either side of her dad, who extended his arms around both of them as they rested their heads on his shoulders. Ryan sat in the back row, monitoring the younger kids, while Toby sat in the row behind Mia.

Toby was happy to have had the honor of meeting Joan a couple of weeks prior to her demise. He recalled their conversation when Mia stepped out to take a call from Winter.

"Toby, Mia is a wonderful young woman. She deserves the best. If you ain't offering that, then don't waste her time. She's already wasted enough with Morris. But if you're going to love her, love her hard with intent and passion, and make sure you always support her goals and her dreams. And I need not say, make sure them babies are raised well, loved, and taken care of. And know that Michael, Mia's father, will hunt you down if you hurt his baby girl. He's ready to kill Morris!"

They enjoyed a laugh. He agreed and promised her that he would be there for Mia, love her, and make every day as special as he could for her, Mylie, and Myles. He intended on keeping his promise.

Jackson walked in, hugged Mia and Leslie, and shook Michael's hand. He walked over and kissed Taryn and Winter on the cheek then kneeled in front of Tanya while keeping Jemarious in his peripheral. He hugged her as tears streamed down both of their faces. She hugged him back, but her embrace was the same as it was for every other person in attendance. He offered his condolences and grabbed a seat in the row adjacent to Taryn and Winter.

***

Tanya, Mia, Winter, and Taryn realigned their seats, and all sat together during the service, holding on to one another for comfort. The funeral director opened the floor for family and friends to pay homage any way they wished.

Winter walked to the front and began to bellow out the words of Boyz II Men, "It's so hard to say goodbye." They all broke down sobbing. Winter had a beautiful voice, and Aunt Joan loved to hear her sing. She paid the perfect homage as she sang out harmoniously.

Then Morris walked Mylie to the front of the room. He held her hand as she recited a poem she had written for her aunt Joan. She cried through the words but managed to get through it. Both Mia and Tanya let out a few squeals once she was done. Mylie ran straight over and wrapped her arms around both of their necks. They embraced her before she walked over and squeezed in between her grandparents and rested her head on her grandmother's lap.

Toby, now seated in the same row, next to Mia, placed his arm across her shoulders as she leaned her head into his chest. Morris rolled his eyes in jealousy as he observed from the back of the room.

Taryn got up and reminisced the funny story about the time when Aunt Joan, Aunt Leslie, and Aunt Tracey ganged up on her, at the age of sixteen, after searching for her until four o'clock in the morning and finally finding her in the backseat of Damion Fuller's BMW. Acknowledging that there were minors in the room, she refrained from giving the details about what she and Damion were attempting to do before they were busted.

"Aunt Joan pulled me out of the car while Aunt Leslie and Aunt Tracey yanked Damion out. They pinned him up against the car and threatened his life if they ever caught him with me again. He pulled off, and he never called me or spoke to me again. Then they all began kicking my behind. I was lumped up by the time they brought me back to my grandparent's house. When my mom opened the door, Aunt Joan knew she was going to knock my behind out, so she jumped in front of me and said, 'No, Michelle! Don't hit her! We found her in the ER. She got jumped at the movies over the young man Damion she was with. Look at these lumps and bruises,' as she pointed to the lumps THEY just put on her. My moms raged turned from me to the girls, whom she'd now believed jumped me. Aunt Joan directed me to go straight to my room and not to bring my you-know-what out for the rest of that weekend. She'd lied to my Mom because she knew it would hurt her to know what I was out doing AND she didn't want me to receive any further corporal punishment than she, Aunt Leslie and Aunt Tracey had already bestowed on me."

The entire room was filled with laughter. Tanya laughed through her tears, recalling the story exactly as Taryn replayed.

Leslie slowly walked to the front. She grabbed Tanya's hand and spoke directly to her. By the end of her speech, she and Tanya were wrapped in a tight embrace. Everyone was sobbing.

Mia couldn't bring her legs to move. She was consumed by her pain and cried into Toby's chest. Her children felt her sorrow, and both went over and tightly embraced her. She leaned into their arms and assured them she'd be OK. As the room cleared, Tanya, Mia, Taryn, and Winter all stayed behind. They held hands and prayed.

Time Heals All Wounds

It's been nearly a year since Mia and Morris finalized their divorce; which commenced couple of months after aunt Joan's passing. Toby and Mia's relationship blossomed. His relationship with Myles and Mylie flourished, and he and Mia began talking about taking things to the next level. Mia was his queen, and he kept his word to her aunt Joan, making every day special for her.

Morris had the kids over his place every other weekend and would have them for a month every summer. He made several attempts to include his new fiancée in their plans, but the kids didn't want any parts of her. Mia and Toby's relationship was now public knowledge around the firm, but they were always extremely professional and never let it get in the way of their work, even when they didn't see eye to eye on work matters.

***

After her mom's funeral, Tanya decided to give Jemarious a fair chance. He was by her side whenever he was in Houston and on the phone with her whenever he had road games. He often flew her to the cities in which he was playing, whenever she didn't have her own business to attend to. She'd realized that he was sincere and genuinely interested in being with her. She hadn't felt so happy in long time and enjoyed every moment with him. The sex was amazing, and he was always the ultimate gentleman, never forgetting his southern roots.

***

Winter and Charlie's love grew exponentially over the past year. He spent practically every weekend at her place. He attended Lacrosse practices and games, ballet and tap rehearsals and recitals, and even participated in Tiffany's father-daughter dance. The twins adored him, and he reciprocated their love. Her second bed-and-breakfast took off much faster than she expected and having Charlie around was a big help for her sanity. She had no idea that he was planning an additional surprise for her soon.

***

Ryan was off to UCLA, while Alana started her new school. Both girls adapted very well to their new home and new life. Chase spoiled them and gave in to every wish they had. Taryn couldn't chastise him because he gave in to all her very own wishes as well. Her charter school thrived, and there was already a wait list for the next cohort of students.

***

Time was beginning to heal all their wounds.

Proposal And More

Chase met Taryn for lunch at her charter school. He brought her favorite salad and a large Diet Coke. He listened and smiled while she raved about her faculty and students. He loved seeing her being so happy and enjoying living out her dream.

He leaned over and whispered in her ear, "I want to be inside of you right now." Her nipples immediately perked up, and she felt a familiar throb between her legs. He continued. "Let's make a quick run home."

Without hesitation, Taryn grabbed her bag and informed her administrative assistant that she'd be taking the remainder of the afternoon off.

Their house was about a thirty-minute drive from the school. Taryn couldn't wait to get home, so she unzipped Chase's pants and began pleasuring his manhood as he drove. He practiced a tremendous amount of self-control as he managed to drive them home safely. However, as soon as they pulled into the garage his pleasure mounted and released.

As they walked into the house, Chase pressed up against her from the back, reached his hands around her, and began to unbutton her blouse, letting it fall to the floor. He then unclamped her bra and allowed that to drop as well. They stopped in the hallway as he pressed her up against the wall and stripped off her suit pants and boy shorts. He stepped back and gave her fully naked body a once over "Damn, babe! Your ass if fine as fuck!"

In her usual sarcastic endearment, Taryn replied, "And you better never forget it."

Chase led her into the bedroom, and to her surprise, there, lying on their bed, were red rose petals in the shape of a heart, with a sky-blue Tiffany box in the center.

Taryn eased over to the bed and grabbed the box, but it was empty when she opened it. She turned around to question Chase and found him on one knee with a five-carat diamond ring in his hand. She looked down at him, and tears began to well up in her eyes. He grabbed her hand, slipped the perfect-sized ring on her finger, and asked, "Taryn, will you spend the rest of your life wit' ya boy?"

Taryn was so choked up, she couldn't get any words out. All she found herself able to do, was nod. Chase stood, wrapped his arms around her waist, kissed her neck softly, and laid her down on top of the rose petals. She felt his muscle fully flexed as he slid himself inside of her. She exhaled as she received all of him and allowed her tears of joy to stream down her face while her husband-to-be made love to her.

"I love you Chase Durr . . .," she whispered in his ear.

No More Secrets

Tanya flew to New Orleans for the weekend. Jemarious secured her a floor seat ticket to his game that Friday and asked her to come out for the weekend. He had a two-day rest before his next game the following Monday and wanted to spend some quality time with 'his girl'. He had a black car pick her up from the airport and escort her to drop her bags at the hotel before bringing her to Smoothie King Arena.

Tanya waltzed into the Ritz-Carlton suite and felt inspired as she took in the stunning French-inspired decorum. She immediately typed up some notes in her phone and e-mailed them to her assistant. She was recently hired to design the home of one of Winter's regular patrons. Although interior design wasn't her main bread and butter, she was just as proficient at it as she was a fashion stylist. She had full creative design over both of Winter's bed-and-breakfast locations, Taryn's office, the library and teacher's lounge at the charter school, and the redesign of Taryn's, Ryan's, and Alana's bedrooms in Chase's house.

She quickly freshened up and changed into a pair of ripped blue jeans, a red-and-black flannel shirt that she tied in a knot at her naval, a pair of all-black Gucci pumps, and a black fedora, which she propped on top of her jet-black curly locks.

Jemarious put on a show that night. He scored nearly forty points. He was happy that Tanya was able to attend the game and see him do his job. She was so good at hers that he wanted to share his very own craft with her. He was, however, exhausted after the game and asked if she was OK going back to the suite and ordering room service. She was a bit drained as well and amicably agreed. They showered, put on some pajamas, ordered in, and watched a movie. They both drifted off to sleep; Jemarious's head on her lap while on the sofa. They both slept unusually late, waking up at approximately 11:00 a.m. on Saturday morning, when housekeeping knocked on the door.

"Good morning, beautiful." He picked his head up and kissed Tanya on the cheek.

"Good morning, you," she responded and continued, "Damn, we must have been tired. Now I'm starving."

Jemarious agreed, and they threw on some sweats and sneakers and headed to Domilise's Po-Boy & Bar for "some banging shrimp po'boys" as Jemarious put it. Turned out he was right. He and Tanya enjoyed their po'boys and a bottle of Corona. When they were done, they hopped in the black car back to the hotel.

"Let's take a walk, J. I want to walk some of these calories off."

Jemarious obliged. The French Quarters was packed as usual. They walked, holding hands and talking. Jemarious curiously invited Tanya to discuss, what he understood, was a very touchy subject for her. He wanted to express his feelings to her but, first, wanted to close the loop on any secrets or unknown knowledge between them.

"T, let's talk serious for a minute. Tell me what really happened between you and that Jackson kid."

Tanya felt comfortable with Jemarious, and she was ready to share this information with him. She needed him to understand why she had concerns about being in another relationship. She began to tell her story.

"Jackson and I met at a basketball game in Harlem. He was my first love. I wasn't a stranger to the street life, which is why it didn't bother me that he was also a street hustler. When I left for college in Chicago, Jackson practically moved out there. He got me an apartment one mile from campus just so he'd be able to stay with me while there. Everything was all good for a while, and I didn't think anything of it whenever Jax was on campus *and* knew more people than both me and Taryn. I figured it was because he often came on campus and played ball with some the team members or in a pickup game."

"One night I was in my room studying when there was a loud knock at the door. I was completely caught off guard when I opened the door to find that it was one of my professors, and he was looking for Jackson. A part of me knew exactly why he was looking for Jax, but I refused to believe it. I didn't even confront him about it. I didn't want to be lied to or, worse, find out the truth."

"Three weeks later, Winter was visiting for the weekend. We had just gotten back to the apartment after drinks at a bar. Taryn was with Ryan's father in her dorm room. She heard the sirens as the police bombarded the campus and entered one of the dormitories. She called my apartment and told Win and I that something was going on, on campus."

"At that exact moment, my apartment door came crashing in, and my place was swarming with police. They threw me and Winter on the floor and handcuffed us while they ransacked my apartment, apparently looking for drugs. Of course, they didn't find anything, and they let us loose. I was so furious because I knew this had something to do with Jackson."

"I was calling his ass like a mad woman, and he wasn't picking up. Little did I know, those same sirens Taryn informed us about were police executing another raid in the dorm room of this chick named Camille. They found two kilos of cocaine in her room. They arrested her immediately. She told the cops the drugs belonged to her "boyfriend," Jackson. Her fucking boyfriend? Seriously?" She paused as she replayed those words in her head then continued, "They couldn't prove anything. Jackson was long gone, back home in New York, while she was being charged with possession and intent to distribute. I did not hear from him for the next three months. No calls. He wouldn't answer my calls or texts. His mother kept telling me she would get my messages to him. Shit, I even sent Mia and Morris on the hunt to look for him in the projects and at Rucker Park. He was M.I.A. I was only able to keep my apartment because I was smart enough to have him advance pay the rent for the entire three and a half years I would be in school."

"However, from that day forward, security watched my every move closely. Then I went to New York to spend the weekend with my mom, and guess who showed up at our door? Yes, mother fuckin' Jackson! He had the nerve to act like everything was OK and that the prior three months hadn't occurred. After I flipped on him, he told me he could not understand why I was so mad. He actually admitted he was fucking Camille and said it was only so that he could use her dorm room as his stash house. He didn't want to put me in any jeopardy by having drugs in my apartment. All I remember doing at that point was smacking the shit out of him, slamming the door in his face, going back inside, and crying in my mother's lap."

"This is why my friends hate him so much, especially Winter. They can't understand how, after a while, I was able to talk to him again. But I'm so done with him. I will never and can never again be in a relationship with him. My mom made me promise her that in our last conversation. I will never break a promise I made to my mother."

Jemarious stopped her in the middle of the sidewalk, faced her toward him, and confessed, "I love you, Tanya, and I promise to never put you through no shit like that."

Big Scare

Winter was having lunch with her staff in the custom lounge she had built as an add-on to the back of her first bed-and-breakfast when she saw the news banner flash across the TV screen. Four officers shot in a shoot-out with local gang members in Walterboro. Three were in critical condition, and one pronounced dead on arrival. Her heart stopped for a second.

Walterboro? Charlie! Oh no. I've gotta call him. She picked up her cell phone and hit Charlie's name on her speed dial. His phone went straight to voice mail. She immediately called again.

Come on, Charlie. Answer the phone.

It went directly to voice mail again. This time, she left a message. "Hey, babe, it's me. I'm looking at the news and see what's going on in Walterboro. I know you're on shift, but I was just checking to see if you're all right. Call me back, please."

Please, God. Don't let this happen again. Winter knew that Charlie's assignment for the day was in Walterboro. He left her that morning, saying he didn't have a good feeling about the day. She felt the panic rise in her chest and asked one of the housekeepers to grab her a bottle of water from the fridge. She tried Charlie's phone again but to no avail; it went straight to voice mail. Then she remembered he had given her his friend Chris's number and told her to try Chris if ever she couldn't directly reach him; he'd be able to get a message to him.

She searched her phone for Chris's number and hit dial. Chris's phone rang three times before he answered. "Detective Chris Swatt here."

Winter was startled by the deep voice on the other end as she was hung up in her worried thoughts.

"Hi, Chris. I mean, Detective Chris. My name is Winter Jones. I am a friend . . . girlfriend . . . his girlfriend . . ." She struggled to get her words out. "Officer Charles Howard. I'm his girlfriend. He gave me your number in the event I was unable to locate him on the job. I know he's working Walterboro today, and I just saw on the news . . ." She couldn't bring herself to repeat the horror she'd heard.

"Yes, Winter! Charlie told me he gave you my number, just in case. I don't want to worry you. I haven't gotten word from Charlie or his partner as of yet. I'm trying to contact him through other means but haven't had much success. Please don't worry. That doesn't mean anything. From what I am gathering, there is still an active shooting exchange involving several gang members and a multitude of officers. Can you stay by the phone? As soon as I know more, I'll give you a call back."

Winter nervously agreed and made sure to turn her ringer up loud to ensure she didn't miss any calls.

My God . . . My God . . . My God, if you love me, please don't let this happen again. Please, God. She walked to her office in conversation with God. When she got upstairs, she picked up her desk phone and called Mia. Mia answered on the first ring.

"Hey, Win. What's up?" At first, there was silence, and Mia could hear Winter breathing deeply into the phone. "Winnn? Winterrr, is everything OK?" She instantly became concerned.

Winter cried into the phone, sharing the situation and her concerns about Charlie.

"Win, please calm down. Let's not expect the worst." Mia tried calming her best friend down.

"Mia, I can't go through this again. The kids cannot go through this again!"

Mia heard the panic in Winter's voice. She knew the traumatic effect Tim's death had on her and the twins and prayed this was not actually happening again. However, she didn't want to add to Winter's worry and tried to remain calm as she talked to her on the phone.

Winter's cell rang while she had Mia on her desk line. It was a number she didn't recognize. She hesitated to answer, fearing the news would be bad. She picked up and heard Charlie's voice on the other line.

"Babe, it's me! I'm OK. My battery died on my cell. I'm so sorry to have you worried. I am out here with the team. We have been able to contain the situation and arrest most suspects involved. Chris was able to get a message to me, and I wanted to give you a quick call to let you know that I'm OK. I'll call you as soon as we get back to the station. Love you, babe!"

Winter felt an overwhelming sense of relief. "Love you too. Make sure you call me back as soon as you get to the station!"

She laid her head back as tears streamed down her face. She had forgotten for a second that Mia was on the line. Mia didn't hang up; she held on as she wanted to be sure she was there for Winter, albeit long distance. Mia silently thanked God for ensuring Charlie's safety and for easing Winter's worries.

Across The State Lines

Mia, Toby, Mylie, and Myles spent the last few weeks house-hunting and had finally settled on a five-bedroom, four-and-a-half-bathroom, Mediterranean style home in Upper Saddle River, New Jersey. They were out at dinner when Toby received the call from the realtor notifying him that the sellers have accepted their offer and were ready to close within the week. Toby was smiling from ear to ear when he hung up the phone.

Mylie loudly squealed out, "We're moving!"

He looked at her and gently pinched the tip of her nose. "Yes. We're moving!"

Mylie clapped her hands in excitement and began chanting, "We're moving! We're moving! We get our own pool! And we get to go to new schools." She laughed and said, "Mommy, that rhymes."

Mia and Toby burst into laughter. Myles was dancing along to Mylie's chant and added, "I get my own basketball court."

Mylie rolled her eyes at Myles and scolded him, "Myles! That does not rhyme."

Mia and Toby laughed even harder. The kids joined them in laughter.

Wedding Bliss

Taryn and Chase's wedding, in the beautiful nook of Tulum, Mexico, was beautiful and intimate, just as she hoped. Everyone was entranced by the lovely sunset backdrop during the ceremony and the luxurious bohemian decor for the reception. She and Chase were head over heels happy and in love. Chase's gaze at his new wife was enchanting. His eyes expressed his genuine love for her. Her best friends felt at peace for her.

***

Charlie and Winter were inseparable. His eyes welled up with tears when he saw her walk down the aisle in her stunning, off white, silk, bridesmaid dress.

I love this woman. I want to spend the rest of my life with her, he thought to himself the entire time he watched her standing there, holding her bouquet of pale pink and white hydrangeas. He held on to her hand for nearly the entire reception dinner, and they floated across the dance floor to every love song that was played.

As the evening festivity was nearing its end, the DJ announced the last song. Charlie whispered in her ear, "Winter, I love you. The best day of my life so far has been the day I caught you in my arms when you fell down the steps of your office." They both laughed at the memory. "But I am looking forward to even better days and ones that will exceed that day."

He paused for a moment, gently moved her back a few inches, and kneeled on one knee. The entire room just stood still. Taryn, Mia, and Tanya were all beaming as they witnessed this beautiful moment for their best friend. Winter was glowing with excitement and joy and genuine surprise at Charlie's gesture. He continued with his unequivocal focus on Winter and not the audience, which he'd drawn.

"Winter Jones. Will you make the best day of my life by becoming my wife?"

Winter stood there for a moment, tears streaming down her face and her heart pounding as loud as bass drums in her chest. She felt like the luckiest woman on earth at that moment. All her fear, anxiety, and doubt were completely washed away, and her heart knew that God sent this man to her. She looked up to the heavens and thanked God and Timmy for giving her this second chance at love and for ensuring that she, Tiffany, and TJ were in good hands.

She glanced down at Charlie with joy in her eyes and happily accepted, "Yes, my love. Yes, I will be your wife!"

After placing the ring on her finger, Charlie stood and embraced her in a passionate kiss. The entire room erupted with applause.

Jemarious and Tanya congratulated Winter and Charlie. "Girllllll . . . I'm so happy for you! You have found you a good man, Win! I love you so much, and you are so deserving of this," Tanya voiced to Winter as she hugged her best friend.

"Charlie, I have no doubt that you'll take good care of my girl and my niece and nephew. Welcome to the family," she said as she gave Charlie a big hug.

Jemarious winked at Winter. "Don't you worry. I got your girl as well."

Winter smiled, knowing he meant that. Tanya looked at him and joked, "You better, or my girls will hunt you down. There won't be any more basketball playing for you."

They all burst into laughter. She then leaned into him and softly kissed him on his cheek and mouthed the words "I love you." He reciprocated.

Mom's Advice

Toby was up at 4:00 a.m., sitting on the balcony of their resort suite, drinking a cup of coffee while talking to his mother on the phone. Toby's parents, Emily and John, were both retired and lived in a lovely cottage in Bronte Country, one of England's most beautiful countrysides. He was an only child and had a very close relationship with them both. He and his mother talked on the phone nearly every other day.

This morning was no exception. However, the topic of discussion was of a serious matter for him, and he wanted his mother's perspective. After all, his parents met and forged their lifelong love after his mother ended an undesirable marriage.

"Mum, I love Mia. She's been through so much, and all I want to do is make her happy. I want to marry her. But after all that Morris put her through, I'm worried that she may not want to be married again." He was genuinely concerned.

"Tobias, Mia knows you love her, and she certainly loves you. She has been fully committed to relocating her and the children to sharing a home with you in the suburbs. That couldn't be an easy decision for her. But because she loves you and knows that you support her career aspirations, which is extremely important to her, she has opened her heart to you. This tells me that she's in for the long haul. I recognize this in her because it's exactly how your father and I came to be where we are today."

Toby smiled at his mother's wisdom. She loved Mia just as much as he did, and she wanted them both to be eternally happy and together.

"You're right, Mum. I'm going to go for it! I love her and want to spend the rest of our lives together." Toby didn't realize that Mia had awaken and overheard his discussion with his mother. She didn't want to interrupt or startle him, so she yawned loudly to alert him that she was awake.

"Mum, Mia's awake, I'll call you later. Love you." Just as he hung up the phone, Mia climbed out of bed and walked straight to him and wrapped her arms around his neck. He cuddled her waist and pulled her close to him.

"Toby. Do you know how much I love you?" she asked, not expecting an answer and continued on, "I would absolutely spend the rest of my life in these arms."

Toby was pleasantly surprised to hear her say those words, yet slightly curious to know if she'd overheard his conversation with his mother. Nonetheless, it didn't matter to him. All that mattered was that she felt the same way he did. Just then, he ran to his luggage and pulled out a red Cartier ring box and walked back over to her. She began jumping up and down in excitement. Toby cracked up laughing at her acting like a kid on Christmas morning after opening their most desired gift.

She ran into his arms, exclaiming, "I love you, Toby! I soooo love you!"

He held her tightly in his arms and spoke softly into in her ear. "Mia Scott, please marry me." Mia responded, "Of course. Yes, Toby, I'll marry you."

Morning Prayer

Mia, Taryn, Tanya, and Winter met in the lobby of their resort at around 10:00 a.m. They'd agreed to meet, just the four of them, so that they could have some time to pray while together. As Mia walked up, Tanya began shouting excitedly, "OMG, Mia! OMG, Mia! What is that I see on your finger?"

Mia was grinning from ear to ear as she lifted her hand and waved it in front of her best friends. "Miaaaaaa!" Taryn shouted with excitement.

"Mia! You too? This is AWESOME!" Winter excitedly exclaimed.

"All y'all chicks getting married. Ummmm, Jemarious better *not* get no ideas. I love him, but ya girl ain't ready for that!"

They all laughed. "Tanya, please. You know you love him and will happily say *yes* when he asks you to marry him," Winter teased and jokingly rolled her eyes.

"True . . . so true! But not just yet. I have *two* weddings to style for. I will be too busy to be planning my own." They all laughed and headed down to the beach.

The four friends stood in a circle, holding one another's hands as they each said their prayer, thanking God for their sisterhood and all that he'd brought them through over the past year. Mia ended her prayer, exclaiming gratefulness to God for a year to exhale.

Printed and bound by PG in the USA